THE TEDDY BEAR MURDERS

JANET HARWARD

Janet Harward lives in the West Midlands with her husband and two daughters. Her first novel *Murder on The English Riviera* was published in 1995, and was followed in 1996 by *The Teddy Bear Murders*, the first Josephine Blake mystery. Her latest novel is *In Memory of Murder*, the second Josephine Blake mystery.

JANET HARWARD

THE TEDDY BEAR MURDERS

Janet Harward

O'Neill Publishing

First published in Great Britain by O'Neill Publishing, 1996.
This edition 1997 O'Neill Publishing.
Copyright © Janet Harward 1996.

A CIP catalogue record for this book is available from the British Library.

ISBN 0-9525161-1-X

9 8 7 6 5 4 3 2 1

Book design and Typography by Crow Media Design.
Printed and bound in Great Britain by Cox & Wyman Ltd, Reading, Berks.

"If you go down to the woods today,
You're sure of a big surprise,
If you go down to the woods today,
You'd better go in disguise.
For every bear, that ever was,
Will gather there for certain
Because today's the day
The teddy bears have their picnic."

Jimmy Kennedy

This book is set in Torbay in Devon. Most district names are genuine. Some places are fictional. The characters and situations are entirely imaginary and bear no relation to any real person or happening.

Dedication

This book is dedicated to the memory of my dear
cousin Diane Dowding

THE TEDDY BEAR MURDERS

Chapter 1

"Hell hath no fury like a woman scorned"
- *William Congreve*

"FOR GOD'S SAKE CAROLINE, I know you're in there, don't get playing silly buggers."

David Vane pressed the bell again and this time he left his finger on for several seconds.

"I'm not going till you answer the door," he shouted through the letterbox again. The door of the next flat opened and an elderly lady in a pink dressing gown with her hair full of curlers stepped out onto the landing.

"Do you know what time it is? My husband's not a well man, it's bad enough the milkman waking him clanging about, but this."

David glanced at his watch. It was a quarter to six in the morning and he suddenly realised he'd been making a din for at least half an hour.

"Oh look, I'm sorry. I just didn't realise the time."

"Had another one of your rows have you? You youngsters, I don't know."

David smiled. He was hardly young... middle-aged more like, he mused. Just at that moment the woman's husband came out looking rather frail and drawn.

"I haven't seen Caroline's car for a day or so, maybe she's away," he said feebly.

"She probably put it in the garage. I know she's in there." He started to shout through the letterbox again.

"You know I haven't seen her for a day or two, perhaps Arthur's right. I mean, she always pops in to see if I want a loaf or anything. She's considerate like that."

"Well, I rang her at work and they said she hadn't been in, but I thought she'd put them up to saying that, just in case I tried to contact her." He looked through the letterbox again and stretched his neck to one side. "Her raincoat's over the chair, I'm sure she's in." He rang the bell again.

"Well if she's got it into her mind not to answer the door, she won't. Maybe she's teaching you a lesson. Look, come in and I'll make some tea. We'll get no sleep now anyway. There's no point going back to bed."

"That's kind of you. It was inconsiderate of me. It's just that I was upset, you know how it is." David let himself be persuaded by Mrs Randall that he needed some decent food inside him. Although he'd insisted he wasn't hungry, he consumed two eggs, three rashers of bacon and a sausage, along with two slices of hot buttered toast finally swilled down with two mugs of tea. The old man looked at him green with envy.

"I wish I could eat like that. I used to have a cast iron stomach but since my ulcer I've to be so careful what I eat. It gets so boring. Boiled fish, mashed potatoes, milky drinks. I can't remember the last time I had a fry-up," he sighed miserably.

"Oh, I like to see someone with a healthy appetite! Anyway, Arthur, at least since I've kept you on the diet the doctor gave me you've had a lot less pain, and your ulcer has settled down."

"I know, but it's so *boring* Doris. I used to love my food."

David had forgotten the problem at hand for a few minutes, listening to the old couple rattle on. He was feeling very tired as he'd been up all night. Suddenly he pulled himself together.

"Well that was lovely Mrs Ryan, thank you, but I must go and try Caroline again".

"I'll tell you what, I've got her mother's number somewhere." She started to mooch through a box of letters. "Here it is."

"Great, I'll give her a call." David went to take the book off her.

"No, I'll ring her. She's not very well and I don't suppose she'll appreciate being woken up this early." She looked over at the clock on the shelf; it was seven forty-five. She dialled the number.

"Oh hello, is that Mrs Stokes? I'm sorry to call you so early. This is Doris Randall, Caroline's neighbour... Oh yes I'm fine thanks Arthur's not too good though. How are you feeling? Oh the arthritis again... I know, it's this damp weather."

David was becoming impatient.

"Hurry up and ask her," he interrupted.

"Actually, the reason I called was to ask you if you'd heard from Caroline... Yes... Oh! And she never turned up you say... Oh no, I don't think there's any cause for alarm. I'll let you know if I find anything out."

She put down the receiver.

"What did she say?" David sounded anxious.

"Well apparently Caroline was supposed to go and see her last night and she didn't arrive. Her mother phoned her but got no reply."

"Well maybe she isn't just avoiding me, perhaps something's happened. I'm going to call the police."

"I don't think she'll like that, it might be nothing... and

yet I suppose she would have contacted her mother if she couldn't make it."

"Precisely. I think something's wrong." He picked up the phone and dialled 999.

Josephine Blake looked into the bathroom mirror. *What a bloody mess!* She thought. Her head was pounding and her eyes looked puffy. She reached for her eye gel. *It's a pity there's no miracle cream for the over-forties*, she thought. She emerged after ten minutes looking slightly more human, after applying her foundation and a couple of coats of mascara. She ran her fingers through her hair. It could have done with a wash but there wasn't time and she couldn't bear the thought of bending her head over the sink with this blinding headache. She made her way to the kitchen, trying to ignore the music that was coming from upstairs. Each beat seemed to be in time with her throbbing temples!

"I can't find any towels. There's none in the airing cupboard!" She tried to ignore the shouts that came from upstairs as she filled the kettle, but she knew she'd have to give in soon. The music went on and on. Josephine stood at the bottom of the stairs.

"Will you turn that bloody row down?"

Her daughter finally gave in and switched off the CD player in the hope of getting a clean towel.

"I don't know why you hide all the towels."

"It's because I'm so sick of them being constantly ruined. That hair colour never comes off and then they're permanently stained. Pour the coffee and I'll fetch you one."

She came back with an old brown towel that she threw

at her daughter.

"For God's sake wipe your face, it's dripping all over the kitchen. I don't know why I bother."

"I didn't think you did."

"Look, that last lounge carpet cost me a fortune, but what with the drinks you and your friends have spilt, it looks like it's been down years, not twelve months. I'm not buying anything new while you're in this house."

"Well you won't have to put up with me much longer if I get a place at Uni."

"Yes well you won't if you don't concentrate more on your A-levels."

"Nag, nag, nag! No wonder dad's gone"

"Your dad has not gone. We're just having a trial separation. There's no-one else involved." Josephine's eyes began to fill up and Jessica felt suddenly very guilty at what she had said. "I know mum, I'm sorry… any more toast?"

She grabbed the old towel and went up to the bathroom to rinse her hair. Josephine sat down thinking how exhausted she felt already and the day had not begun yet. She and her daughter seemed to clash constantly lately. Maybe she should perhaps take her doctor's advice and go on the HRT. What with the pressures of the job and everything, she knew Tom felt he was being neglected, but what about her? She could not help the stresses and strains of her job. She needed him to listen and understand too. He was being selfish. They needed a break. She realised that. So he had gone to stay with his mother. But what if he turned to someone else for comfort and sex? They had always had a good sex life, but lately she was so tired. What if he did meet someone? She suddenly felt panicky and sick inside. She had never bothered with anyone, her job was too demanding, but he might. She was suddenly brought back down to earth by the sound of her daughter's voice.

"Mum are you all right? Look at the time."

"Oh my God, it's ten to nine!" She gulped down her coffee and ran upstairs to change.

The police car drew up outside Kew Gardens, a development of three storey flats situated in pleasant gardens just outside Torquay. The two PCs went up to the second floor where David Vane and Mrs Randall were waiting for them. David quickly explained that he was a friend of Caroline Ryan, and that no one had been able to contact her for a day or so and he was rather worried. After determining that the flats did not have a caretaker with a master key, the young PC Richards spoke to his colleague and they agreed they'd have to break down the door. After several minutes they gained access to flat number fifteen. The flat was cold and felt uninhabited.

Checking each room in turn they eventually came to the bedroom. PC Richards opened the door and entered. Opposite him the body of a woman in a nightie was propped up on a chair against the wardrobe door in a sitting position. Her face was blue and contused; her purple tongue protruded grotesquely. She looked like a child's doll that had been clumsily posed. Her long blonde hair cascaded over her shoulders, partly obscuring the bow at the side of her neck, made from the tights that had been used to strangle her. Next to her sat a teddy bear with a blue ribbon around its neck, tied in the same fashion. The young PC flinched from the sight and tried to move backwards to block the door. Too quickly Vane came up behind him and took in the scene before him. It was like his worst nightmare; surely he would wake up any moment now. He felt a welling sensation inside him and an overwhelming feeling of nausea he'd never experienced before. He turned round, but before he could reach the bathroom he vomited all over the hall carpet.

"I told you not to give him that big breakfast," the old man said as he went back to his flat.

Detective Inspector Josephine Blake sat at her desk. The paperwork seemed never ending as she sifted through it lethargically.

"If we didn't have so much of this time-consuming rubbish, perhaps we could get on with the real job. Mind you, when we do finally get them to court, some smart-arse lawyer gets them off on a technicality. So all our hard work is a waste of time. Still, I suppose the mountains of paperwork keep us so occupied we don't realise how pointless it all is."

"My, we're depressed today, aren't we ma'am?" The young Detective Constable Roger Barnes smiled.

"Just stating facts Barnes. Any news on that stabbing from forensic?"

"Well the blood group of the victim matches the blood found on the tee-shirt of the suspect, and they were heard arguing. I think he was trying to muscle in on the victim's patch. That could be one more drugs dealer off the streets—well two if you include the victim."

"Yes Barnes. There'll be someone else just waiting to step into their shoes. It goes on and on. When I joined the force as a young WPC I thought we were here to help in the fight to stop crime. God, I was young and idealistic then. Now I realise we can only get rid of a bit of the vermin here and there. As you know, rats breed."

"Surely the drug situation wasn't so bad in the sixties?" DC Barnes said.

"It wasn't. There was cannabis, speed and LSD, but nothing like the stuff that's out there today. It's out of control now."

The office door opened and Detective Sergeant Hughes entered.

"There's a suspicious death at a flat in Barton. Here's the address. It looks like a case for CID."

He handed Josephine a piece of paper with the address on. She glanced at it for a moment or two.

"Okay Sergeant… you come too Barnes, and get DC Fletcher. The experience will be good for her."

As she sat in the back of the car Josephine decided to apply a coat of lipstick. She still felt bare without it but she'd been in such a rush that morning. She opened her compact and looked at her hair in its mirror, wishing she had washed it. She was an attractive forty-three year old woman with short ash blonde hair, but she looked her age. The late nights and the pressures of the job had taken their toll, and it showed. Her blue eyes were lined with dark circles, but still retained a certain appeal and sparkle. In her youth she had thought her eyes her best feature. She had joined the force as a young PC and had taken a few years off when Jessica was small. When she returned to the force it had been an uphill struggle to get to the rank of Detective Inspector. She'd had a lot of opposition and resentment from her male colleagues and there were days when she had felt like jacking it all in. But Josephine was a survivor. She had managed the balancing act of being a wife, mother and career woman, but lately she'd felt herself slipping off the tightrope. The pressure had been the cause of much of the tension in her marriage. Tom still loved her, there was no doubt about that: he just needed time to sort things out. Her transfer to CID three years previously had been a fair success although the last two murder cases had been drug related so she had worked closely with the drug squad. Those crimes always depressed her. She never felt any remorse for the murdered drug dealers. As far as she was concerned they had got their just rewards. It was the thought of so many young people damaging their bodies and minds that really got to her.

The car drew up on the drive at Kew Gardens and they went up to the flat. forensic and the two PCs were there. PC Richards came up to her.

"Any witnesses?" she asked.

"Not really. The victim's boyfriend and neighbours are in the flat next door; apparently they had been trying to contact her."

"Okay, I'll speak to them later." She went into the bedroom where Caroline Ryan's body was propped upright. Josephine Blake felt a little trembly when she saw the deformed expression on the victim's face. She took control of herself. "What a waste! I should think she was quite a pretty woman, despite the way she looks now. Only in her thirties I'd guess." She looked closely at the tights tied in a bow at the side of her neck.

"I wonder if these were used to strangle her and then the murderer tied them in this fashion. I suppose forensic will let us know."

"Whoever the sick bastard was that did this he couldn't have been in a hurry to get away, or panicked, to have gone to the trouble of tying such a neat bow." Sergeant Bill Hughes commented.

"I wonder if the teddy bear belonged to the victim or whether the murderer left it." Josephine turned to the Sergeant.

"Well I should think it was hers. I mean, you women like soft toys don't you, no matter what age you are? I mean, my wife's got a toy dog at the end of our bed... the silly bugger. I can't see a murderer carrying a teddy bear around with him, can you?" he smirked.

"Oh I don't know... you men never grow up," she replied. Just at that moment the forensic pathologist arrived.

"Hello, Detective Inspector Blake isn't it?" He shook her hand "I don't think we've met before. I'm John Gardner... Oh hello Bill, I didn't see you there. How's the family?"

"Fine thanks."

He went over and examined the body for several minutes.

"I can't tell you much till I get her back to the path lab, but at a guess I'd say she's been dead about twenty-four hours."

"Do you think that the tights around her neck killed

her?" Very carefully with his gloved hand he pulled the tights a little away from her neck.

"From the bruising on her neck and the way they're tied I'd say yes, but I'll give you a full report later." Josephine turned to DC Roger Barnes.

"Get the place checked thoroughly with the forensic team to see if there is any sign of a break in or struggle, although everything seems in order. Still if the murderer was meticulous enough to tie that bow they probably tidied up after them." She turned to the PC. "Was there any damage to the front door before you broke it down?"

"No ma'am. Whoever it was certainly didn't gain entry there," he replied. She walked over to the closed window and looked down.

"Well there's no trellis or balcony so I doubt if anyone could have got in this way. It's quite a way down unless the murderer used a ladder, which is unlikely. I think we can only assume at this point that she let the murderer in."

"Get me the reports on your findings as soon as you can." she told the forensic team.

"Come along Bill we'll go and talk to the boyfriend." She shouted over to John Gardner "I'll see you at the Lab after the post-mortem to go through the report with you."

"All right, that's fine," he turned to Sergeant Hughes.

"It's okay she likes to be on the spot all the time." Bill said quickly. Josephine stood at the door of the flat.

"Are you coming Sergeant?" She snapped. He followed her wondering whether she had overheard him. As they entered flat number seventeen David Vane was sitting in the lounge with Doris and Arthur Randall. He looked up. His eyes were red and swollen. Josephine went over to him.

"I'm Detective Inspector Blake and this is Detective Sergeant Hughes. I believe you're the deceased's boyfriend?"

"Yes, that's right," David Vane stammered a little. He took a deep breath. "I'm sorry… it was such a shock. I've been trying to contact her."

"Yes I'm sure it's upsetting for you. Take your time," Josephine reassured him.

"Would you like some tea?" Doris asked.

"Yes … that would be lovely," Josephine smiled. "Now, when did you last see Caroline Ryan?"

"Well let's think… What's today's date?"

He seemed confused.

"It's Friday 2nd June," the Sergeant informed him.

"Let's see, we went out on Monday night for a meal. We had a terrible row and Caroline stormed out of the restaurant."

"And what time was that?" Hughes asked, as he was taking notes.

"Well let's see … the table was booked for nine. I suppose about ten o'clock, but I'm not sure. Anyway that same evening I came around to patch things up at about eleven-thirty."

"And was she in?"

"Yes, she answered the door to me, and told me to go away… well her exact words were 'piss off you chauvinist pig,' and she slammed the door in my face."

"Did you try to contact her again?"

"Yes I called her again on Tuesday and she answered the phone, but when she knew it was me she slammed it down. I also contacted her at work."

"What day was that?"

"Wednesday. They said she wasn't there, but I think she was and wouldn't come to the phone."

"We'll check it out. Where did she work?"

"Exclusive Windows in Paignton. She was a secretary. I've got the phone number somewhere." He got out a little book and gave them the number. Josephine continued.

"So what happened then?"

"Well I just had to speak to her. I decided to come to the flat early, I arrived at about five-thirty this morning. I thought if I made a noise she would let me in so as not to disturb the neighbours. But she didn't answer the door because she couldn't." He put his head in his hands.

"But you did wake us up." Doris said as she put the tea on the table. As they drank the tea Sergeant Hughes said, "Oh by the way, I noticed these flats have a row of garages. Did Caroline Ryan have a car?"

"Yes she had a blue Metro."

Doris Randall interrupted. "Actually Inspector, Arthur was saying he hadn't seen her car for a day or two, but it might be in the garage I suppose."

"Do you know where she kept the garage key?" Josephine asked David.

"I think it's on the same key-ring as her door key."

"Get them to check the flat for her keys when we're finished will you Sergeant?"

"How long have you known Mrs Ryan. Or is it Miss Ryan?" DS Hughes asked.

"Well she's divorced but she kept her married name. I think at work she was known as Miss Ryan... We've been going out for about nine or ten months."

"And did you have lots of rows?" Josephine asked.

"No more than any other couple."

"Was she seeing another man?" David looked shocked.

"Oh no... I don't think so! I mean I used to see her about five nights a week and she used to visit her mother once a week. The other night she went to an aerobics class. No, I'm sure she wasn't."

"Can you think of anyone that might want her dead?"

"No... no-one at all," he raised his voice. "I thought it was a burglar."

"Well how would he get in? You couldn't gain access at the front door, the windows haven't been touched and there doesn't appear to be anything missing. It's early days but we think perhaps, Caroline knew her murderer, or at least let them in herself. Do you know who is her next of kin?" Josephine asked David.

"She didn't have any children and she doesn't see her ex-husband now. There's a sister, but I don't know her address."

"Oh my God," Doris jumped up.

"What?"

"Her poor mother doesn't know yet. I rang her this morning to ask if she had heard from Caroline. Apparently last night she was supposed to go for a meal but she didn't arrive."

"Have you got her mother's address?"

"Yes I'll get it for you." Doris scuttled out of the room.

"You can go and see the mother Bill."

"Don't you think it needs a woman's touch?"

"Take DC Fletcher with you, she needs the experience. You can have the car and I'll go back in the squad car."

"Shall I call them?"

"No, I've not finished here yet." The sergeant left the flat.

"Can you tell us anything about her circle of friends?" Josephine asked David Vane.

"Well we met at a local Divorced and Singles club. I can give you the name of the place. She had a couple of girlfriends she went out with before."

"And do you still go?"

"Oh yes. I mean, it's a good place. The music's not too loud and there's a nice bar. I mean Caroline has lots of friends there, men and women. She still sees them. I mean even if you're going out with someone, you should still keep in touch with friends, don't you think?"

"Yes I agree," Josephine replied. She thought for a moment that might have been her own trouble. She had lost touch with a few good friends because of her job. She had colleagues in the police force, but it wasn't the same. *I wonder if I'll end up going to a Divorced and Singles club if Tom and I split up permanently. I suppose there's a lot of lonely people about.* David Vane interrupted her thoughts.

"Anything else?" he asked.

"Oh… no, thank you Mr Vane. If you leave your name and we may need to question you further." Just as she was about to leave the flat she turned suddenly.

"Oh, by the way I nearly forgot. Did you see the teddy bear that was left next to Caroline's body?"

"No I didn't notice, it was such a terrible sight. I was horrified. I'm afraid I was sick all over the hall carpet."

"Well, there was a teddy bear. Can you come back in with me and take a look?"

"I don't know… the sight of her body…"

"It will be covered now," she assured him. As they entered the flat the forensic team had just finished taking photographs of the body and they pulled up the zip of the black body bag. Josephine pointed to the teddy bear.

"I've never seen it before."

"Are you sure?"

"Yes, I mean I've slept here several times. I'm sure it's not Caroline's."

"Okay thank you, we'll be in touch."

He looked very sad and tired.

"I know we've rowed this last week, but I really thought a lot of her. It's lonely out there when you're divorced or separated. We're all looking for someone and I thought I'd found her."

"Then perhaps you could go back to the club where you met to see your friends."

"I don't think I'll bother again," David looked hurt and depressed as he walked out.

I know how he feels, Josephine thought. She went back to Doris and Arthur's flat.

"I didn't catch your surname," she said to Doris.

"It's Randall, Mr and Mrs Randall."

"I'll send my detective constable to see you to take a statement and if there's anything else you remember please contact me. Here's my number," she handed Doris a card. As she took it Doris felt very important.

"Oh yes. I will Inspector, thank you."

Probably a bit of excitement for them. Josephine thought. *Mind you she seems a bit of a busybody. Still that's not a bad thing; most pensioners get a bit bored, and seem to notice who is coming and going. I'll get Barnes to ask her if anybody's called at the flat lately. She's bound to remember something.*

"Almost finished here ma'am." DC Barnes informed her.

"That's good, DC Fletcher's gone with Sergeant Hughes to see the mother. I'll go back with PC Richards. I want you to take a statement from the neighbours, Mr and Mrs Randall. The old man seems a bit frail but she is the type that wouldn't miss a thing."

"Okay ma'am. By the way we've found the car keys: it's garage number five." He handed them to her. She walked down with one of the forensic team. They opened the door and the blue Metro was there. She jotted down the registration number.

"Check the car over and report back to me."

Detective Inspector Josephine Blake had been back at the station about for an hour when DS Hughes returned with DC Sally Fletcher.

"The mother was extremely upset. She kept asking us how and why and we didn't have any answers for her. I felt so sorry." DC Fletcher said.

"I know it's sad, but the only thing we can do for her now is to find her daughter's murderer." Josephine replied.

"We've got a statement," DS Hughes looked through his book. "Her daughter had arranged to visit her at about seven thirty, and she was going to cook a meal for her as she thought her daughter wasn't eating properly."

"Was she going straight from work?"

"Well her mother said as far as she knew, Caroline was going home first to shower and change. She normally got home at six."

"And what time did her mother try to contact her?"

"Well apparently when she never arrived she waited till about eight-thirty and rang her daughter but got no reply."

"Was she worried?"

"Well not unduly. Apparently Caroline wasn't the best of timekeepers."

"Do you think she's right about the time? I mean, she's quite elderly," Josephine asked.

"Oh yes, ma'am," DC Fletcher said. "I mean she's only about sixty, quite a smart looking woman."

"Oh... I don't know why I expected her to be older. Still, I suppose if Caroline Ryan was say about mid-thirties, then her mother might easily be about sixty. I seem to think everyone's mum is the same age as mine." She stopped to think for a moment or two and then continued. "Let us assume something was obviously wrong otherwise she would have contacted her mother. We don't have the exact time of death till we get the results from the post-mortem, but the body was examined by the pathologist at say about eight o'clock. So if his guess is right about her being dead around twenty-four hours, that would put the time of death any time between seven and nine p.m. the previous evening."

"I asked Mrs Stokes if she knew any of her daughter's friends. Apparently she had met David Vane and found him charming. She also gave us the names of two close friends, although she didn't have their telephone numbers." DS Hughes informed her.

"Right send DC Barnes back to Kew Gardens to see if there is an address book in the flat anywhere. Arrange to have the residents in the flats questioned to see if anyone saw or heard anything or anyone that may have looked suspicious. Let's get the teddy bear checked out to see where it came from. Did either you or DC Fletcher ask the mother if Caroline Ryan had a teddy bear?" There was a silence.

"No, I didn't think you had. Phone her, will you Fletcher?" She turned round to face DS Hughes

"Would you fetch us both some sandwiches and tea from the canteen Bill and then we'll go to Caroline Ryan's workplace. Something Windows wasn't it?" She looked through some notes on her desk. Just at that moment DC Barnes came into the room.

"Excuse me ma'am, but the Chief Superintendent wants a word."

"Thanks Barnes, I'll be there in a moment."

"She's had me running around all day," Bill moaned as he waited for his tea in the canteen.

"Well, it is a murder inquiry Sarge," the young DC replied.

"I know, but DC Fletcher could have interviewed the mother alone, but the DI insisted I held her hand."

"Well Fletcher hasn't been in CID very long, you couldn't really let her go alone. What was the woman like who was murdered?"

"Oh her face looked terrible… all blue and deformed… you know how they look after strangulation. She had a nice body though and long blonde hair. Probably asked for it though… you know what these women are like?"

He suddenly felt a sharp dig in his back.

"No, I don't as it happens but I'm sure you'll educate me!" DC Fletcher said angrily. He hadn't realised she had come up behind him. When she left the canteen the DC asked DS Hughes

"What's wrong with her then?"

"Probably that time of the month," DS Hughes replied.

"My word Bill, you're a bigger chauvinist than me!"

Chapter 2

THE DRIVER took Josephine Blake and the Sergeant to Exclusive Windows. A rather nervous looking secretary quickly showed them in to the Managing Director.

"Nothing wrong I hope?" she kept asking, as she showed them into Mr Sullivan's office. They introduced themselves to him and produced their identity cards.

"Mr Sullivan, I believe you have an employee named Caroline Ryan?" DS Hughes asked.

"Yes she's one of our secretaries… do you need to speak to her? I can get my secretary to fetch her." He reached for the phone.

"I'm afraid that would be impossible Mr Sullivan. You see, Caroline Ryan has been found murdered."

The managing director looked shocked.

"Are you sure? I mean Caroline… I was only talking to her the other day."

"Yes, there's no doubt I'm afraid."

"Oh, I know that was silly thing to say; it's just that it's such a shock." He regained his composure and the Inspector continued.

"How long has Miss Ryan worked for you?"

"Well I'm not sure of the exact dates, but I think she may have been with us for two or three years."

"Do you know of any problems she may have had?"

"No, not really, but I think you'd better talk to her colleagues. I mean, I like to try to keep in touch with my staff but a lot of people seem to distrust and shy away from management."

I know the feeling Josephine thought.

"Well could we speak to her work colleagues. How many are there?"

"She shared an office with another secretary, Mrs Colgan, and their section leader Mr Wright. You can interview them in here if you want to. I've got to check on something anyway."

"That would be easier thank you," the Sergeant replied.

"Perhaps you would like some tea or coffee?"

"Yes, tea thank you," Josephine replied.

"Right then," he stood up hesitantly and pressed his buzzer. "Oh Kate, can you send Mr Wright up to my office and arrange for some tea."

The interview with Caroline Ryan's section leader Mr Wright proved quite fruitless. He was the type who lived for the job, and didn't really socialise with the staff or enquire about their private life at all. The only information they got from him was that Caroline Ryan was reasonably good at her job and a bit of a gossip. Apparently she and Mrs Colgan were always having 'cosy little chats' and he often had to tell them to get on with their work. The only thing he knew about her was that she was divorced. They thanked him for his assistance and as he was leaving he was asked to send Mrs Colgan to the office to see them.

"Well he was a bit of a waste of time, unless he knows more than he makes out."

The Sergeant poured himself another cup of tea.

"Still if what he says is true about Caroline Ryan always gossiping with Mrs Colgan, she might be more helpful," Josephine remarked.

"She sounds like the regular grapevine," Sergeant Hughes said smugly.

"Not necessarily. Women just tend to have more friends than men."

"Do you think so? Most men have mates they play football with, and drinking buddies."

"Yes but that's all you talk about. Drink, sex and football. Women confide more in one another," Josephine replied. Just at that moment there was a knock on the door and Jean Colgan entered. She was an attractive looking woman of about forty-five with dark hair styled in a bob. Although she had put on a fresh coat of lipstick, her eyes were red and her mascara was slightly smudged.

"Please take a seat Mrs Colgan." She sat down nervously.

"Call me Jean, please"

"Would you like some tea?" Josephine asked, "though I think it may be a bit cold now."

"Oh… no I'm fine thanks," her voice sounded trembly. She tried to keep her composure but suddenly broke down and started to cry. Josephine gave her a tissue and after a few minutes Mrs Colgan seemed to take control.

"I'm sorry, it's just that we were quite good friends, not just work mates… and it's such a shock! I mean all we've been told is that she was found dead in her flat. I mean it wasn't a heart attack was it? Surely she was too young?"

"We're from the CID and are treating this as a murder inquiry."

"Murdered? Was she attacked… raped… what? Was it a burglar? I told her she didn't have enough security."

She started to cry again. Sergeant Bill Hughes was very impatient.

"Caroline Ryan was found strangled and there were no signs of a break-in. We could assume it was someone she knew." Josephine gave him a stern glance. She turned to the woman.

"Look Jean, I know this must be a terrible shock for you, but you may be able to help us."

"Oh yes… I mean anything I can do."

"You say you were good friends. Did you go out together?"

"Oh yes, on the odd night she didn't see David," she replied.

"So you knew her boyfriend?"

"Yes. I was with her the night they met."

"Tell us everything you can about Caroline. Take your time, the Sergeant will take notes."

"Well, we had worked together for about two years. Our boss Mr Wright didn't seem to like us having a chat at work, bit of a slave driver he is. Not a bad boss though I suppose. One night we went out for a drink after work and we've been firm friends ever since."

"Can you tell us anything about her ex-husband?"

"Mark Ryan? Let's think… they had been married about eight years."

"So Caroline still kept her married name?"

"Yes. She just called herself Miss Ryan after the divorce."

"Do you think her ex would want to do her any harm?"

"I think it started out as a bit of a stormy divorce but they eventually reached quite an amicable settlement. They sold the house and split the money. Of course there were no children involved. It's always more awkward when there are… don't you agree?"

"I certainly do," Josephine sighed, thinking of the problems she was having with Jessica.

"You were saying about the divorce," Bill urged her to continue.

"Oh yes… well as I was saying… Caroline bought the flat out of her half of the settlement and they ended up quite good friends… well as friendly as you can be after a divorce. In fact the last I heard he was living with someone else. He may even be married now."

"Did Caroline keep in touch with him?" Josephine asked.

"I don't think she saw him socially but she sent him a card at Christmas and birthdays, that sort of thing. She used to visit his mother occasionally. They were quite close when she and Mark were married. I think she could always ring Mark up in an emergency… say a burst pipe or something like that. Although since she had been going out with David, he did any odd jobs around the flat."

"How was their relationship?"

"They had been going out for about twelve months or thereabouts. I should say they got on quite well."

"So you don't know anything about this recent argument? Apparently he was trying to contact her but she was avoiding him."

"I knew they'd had a row, but they were always arguing."

"But you just said they got on quite well." The sergeant sounded confused.

"They had a lot of silly rows, none of them serious— they'd always make up. Caroline would just keep David sweating for a day or two. It was all part of the game. I think they actually enjoyed quarrelling."

Sergeant Hughes shrugged his shoulders. He clearly didn't understand. Josephine could relate to what she was saying. She and Tom used to thrive on a good row and in the early days the making up was the best part. This recent break-up when Tom had gone to live with his mother was out of character. They had become indifferent to one another lately. There was no arguing, they had just grown further apart.

"So you don't think he could have murdered Caroline?" Sergeant Hughes' question brought her back to reality. Jean Colgan shuddered.

"Do you know I'd almost forgotten she's dead." She paused for a moment. "No. I'm sure David couldn't possibly do a thing like that," she said adamantly.

"You say you were with her the night she met David. Where was that?" Josephine asked.

"We used to go to a Divorced, Singles and Separated Club called the Blue Forest," she replied.

"So you're divorced too, Mrs Colgan?" Sergeant Hughes asked.

"Well no, actually I'm happily married," Jean said unashamedly. "You see it's a good night out. We have a drink and dance with the girls. There aren't many clubs nowadays for our age group. They just seem to cater for the youngsters. The Blue Forest Club plays lots of '50s, '60s, '70s music not all this head banging rubbish the discos and pubs play now. When you go to a pub with the youngsters you feel so old but the age group at the Blue Forest varies from thirty-five to sixty."

"And do you have a relationship with another man?" the sergeant asked.

"No, I don't, and even if I did it wouldn't be any of your business! As I've already said, I'm happily married. I just go about once every two or three weeks to have a laugh with the girls."

I think I'll have to join you one week, Josephine thought to herself. She rather liked Jean Colgan but thought that perhaps she was being just a little too friendly with her. This was possibly a fault of hers when interviewing, although sometimes it had proved to be an advantage, the softer approach, rather than being too aggressive. Some people would open up more.

"We're not here to offend but we do have to ask these questions Mrs Colgan. This is a murder investigation and obviously as she was your friend I'd have thought that you, as much as anyone, would want us to try and find out who murdered her."

"Oh yes... I see that... I'm sorry I snapped." She turned her head to the sergeant in the way of an apology. "I'm just still shocked and upset."

"Well that's understandable," he replied.

"Now, are there any other friends we can contact?" Josephine asked. "Yes. I'll give you the names of the two girls who we go with."

"So Caroline still went there?"

"Well yes. Most of the time with David, sometimes without him. As I say, although she met him there it was a good club, people still went as couples." She wrote down the address and telephone number of the other two friends and handed them to Josephine.

"Thank you. Now if you can think of any other information please contact me. Ask for Detective Inspector Blake or Detective Sergeant Hughes." She gave Jean Colgan the number. "Oh, and one other thing. Did Caroline have a teddy bear do you know?"

"No. I've never seen one in her flat... why?"

"A bear was found next to her body."

"Maybe David bought it for her," Jean suggested. "Okay, that will be all for now thank you." Jean Colgan left the office.

As they got back into the car Josephine said to the driver. "You can drop me off in town on the way back to the station, I've got some dry-cleaning to collect."

"Yes certainly ma'am."

"Mind if I smoke?" Bill Hughes lit a cigarette before either of them had a chance to reply. "Do you believe all that about her just going out for a night with the girls and being happily married?" he asked Josephine.

"Yes I do, actually, Bill. She probably just needs a break from her husband and a few laughs. Maybe if I'd done that when the job was getting to me I wouldn't have the problems I've got now."

"Well I certainly wouldn't like my wife going to a place like that."

"When did you last take your wife out Bill?" she asked. "We went for a meal on her birthday."

"Is that it? You're always going to the pub when your shift's finished or the local football match."

"Well I need a drink with the stress of this job, I mean it's so bloody dangerous. Do you remember when I collared that drugs dealer and he pulled that knife on me? If I hadn't got the boot in when I did I'd have been dead meat, and you begrudge me going out for a drink with the lads!" He tried to justify himself.

"I'm simply saying, Bill, that maybe your wife needs a break as well," Josephine said. She knew she'd got his back up and was quite enjoying it.

"Just let me out here," she said to the driver as he drove around the harbour. "I'll see you back at the station Bill." Just as she got out of the car she said teasingly "I think I'll try that Divorced and Singles club if Tom and I don't get back together. Ask Mary if she would like to come with me for a night out."

"Over my dead body," was his reply. "Don't say things like that and tempt fate Sergeant." Josephine laughed as she slammed the car door.

Detective Chief Inspector Cunningham entered the incident room. "Hello Sergeant, is Detective Inspector Blake about anywhere?"

"She had to drop off in town sir. I don't think she will be long though."

"Would you ask her to come and see me when she returns? Nothing on this murder case yet at Kew Gardens I suppose?" he asked.

"Well we've interviewed her employer, and work colleagues... then there's the boyfriend seems okay but you never know. We'll know more when we get something back from forensic," Bill informed him.

"Chase them up and get DI Blake to give me a full report tomorrow. I think I'll get off now, I've a few things to do."

"Will do sir." As he left Bill turned to DC Fletcher.

"I suppose he's going to get a round of golf in. I'm off to the canteen, see you later."

"Okay Sarge."

When DI Blake returned DC Fletcher told her about Chief Inspector Cunningham wanting the low-down on the case.

"Well we haven't much to go on till we get the report

from forensic," Josephine said.

"Actually ma'am that's what DS Hughes told him. I think he was trying to get him off your back. You have got to go and see him tomorrow."

"Good old Bill. Maybe I've been a bit too hard on him lately. By the way where is he now?"

"Down at the canteen I think ma'am."

"Can you get him and DC Barnes to come to the incident room and we'll go through what we've got so far." When they were all assembled in the incident room, DI Blake started to speak.

"Well, we've got the boyfriend David Vane. Any views on him?"

"Well he seems a decent sort, and he was concerned enough to contact us," DS Hughes remarked.

"Yes, but we still don't know much about him, and remember there were no signs of a break-in. I think we can assume it was someone she knew," she continued. "We have Jean Colgan's statement. DS Hughes you can… no I've changed my mind, DC Fletcher can check out her other friends. I'll give you their addresses."

"That's a pity, they might be available if they go to the Divorced and Single Club! Are you sure you don't want me to go ma'am?"

"No. They might confide more in a woman." Josephine replied. "Barnes, contact the two PCs that are interviewing all the occupants at Kew Gardens to see if they have managed to find anything out, and Bill… "

"Yes ma'am."

"You can go and talk to the ex-husband although I believe she hadn't seen him for a while. Now, anyone got any views on this teddy bear? Rather bizarre if the murderer did leave it there."

"Could it just have been a coincidence?" DC Barnes suggested.

"Well not with the tights tied in a bow around her neck like the teddy bear," Josephine remarked.

"Bit of a joker then this chap, don't you think?" Bill said.

"We're assuming it was a man who murdered her but we don't know yet if there was any sexual interference." Josephine looked at her watch. "Four o'clock. I think I'll have time to go down to the forensic lab and see what they've got for us."

"Ah DI Blake… nice to see you even though it is a little late in the day."

John Gardner smiled.

"Not the hours I work it's not," Josephine added.

"Do you want to see the body?" he asked a little hesitantly.

"Of course! It amazes me the way you think all women are squeamish. I'd say it's the other way round, the number of men I've seen pass out in labour rooms."

He removed the sheet from Caroline Ryan's body.

"She doesn't look as bad now as when we found her all blue and deformed. She must have been quite a pretty girl," he remarked. "As you can see there are marks on her wrists and a small bruise on her temple. I think this indicates that there was some sort of struggle."

"Would the bruise on her temple have caused her to pass out?" Josephine asked.

"I think she may have knocked her head on the side of

the wardrobe, which may have given her slight concussion. That would have caused her to feel faint and would have given her assailant an advantage when strangling her, as she probably wouldn't have been able to defend herself."

"The body was found at about eight-thirty by the two PCs this morning."

"Well she had been dead about twelve hours. So I'd put the time of her death roughly between eight and nine p.m. on Thursday evening." John Gardner informed her.

"We'll have to find out where the boyfriend was at around that time."

"I shall put in my report that death was caused by strangulation and the tights that were tied in a bow round her neck were those that were used to strangle her. But one thing I did notice that you may think interesting, is that there was no sexual interference."

Josephine thought for a minute and then said

"So this wasn't done in a fit of rage. I mean surely the murderer would panic and just want to flee the scene of the crime. Why bother with the teddy bear or tying the bow?"

"She was in good health, and the contents of her stomach were a cheese sandwich and quite a quantity of red wine."

"She was supposed to be going to her mother's for a meal. So she could have eaten a quick snack, although I can't understand her drinking the wine, especially since she was supposed to dine at her mother's. I wonder if she was drinking wine with her murderer before he or she turned on her, which would support the fact that she knew them," she suggested.

Chapter 3

HE NOTICED the attractive redhead at the end of the bar looking his way and couldn't believe his luck. All night he'd been watching her and wondering what a great pair of legs she'd got and the short red mini skirt she was wearing showed them at their best.

He decided to make a move.

"Can I buy you a drink Miss?" He enquired.

"Yes thank you dry white wine."

"Do you live here?" he continued.

"Not far and you?"

"I've come down to Devon for some work a mate promised me, but unfortunately nothing came of it so I'm heading back to the Midlands tomorrow."

"Oh that's a shame, I hope you're not disappointed with the place."

"No Torquay's lovely. I just wished I could have stayed longer."

After a couple of drinks she became friendlier, and began to rub her knee against his leg.

"Would you like to go out anywhere I mean I don't know the area, but are there any good clubs?"

"We don't want to go to any smoky packed club, do we? I can think of something much better," she took his hand.

"I'm easy, whatever you want to do."

He nipped into the gent's toilet and was relieved to see a condom machine, he sorted out some change and put it in the machine. He didn't like wearing the things. Still better be safe than sorry, he thought to himself.

It was a clear evening, with a full moon. The woods

were desolate and although the ground was soft he would have preferred to have sex in the car, even though it would have been cramped.

As she started to remove her blouse and skirt, he got more aroused and his penis became rigid.

As he unzipped his trousers, and they fell to the floor, his expression changed from one of lustful anticipation to utter terror and panic as he looked up at the horrendous spectacle before him.

"God help me!" he shrieked.

His cries of terror ceased as the wooden log hit him on the head with such an impact that it crushed his brain instantly.

Chapter 4

THE FOLLOWING DAY they were all assembled in Detective Inspector Blake's office.

"I went to see the ex-husband Mark Ryan yesterday at Plymouth. It's much quicker now they've finished the new motorway." Bill said stirring his coffee.

"Was he upset?" DI Blake asked.

"I think he was, although he didn't show it. The woman he's living with was there too. Apparently they're getting married in September so he probably didn't want her to think that he still had feelings for his ex-wife."

"That's very observant and sensitive of you Bill... getting soft in your old age?" Josephine said teasingly.

"Did you ask him his whereabouts on Thursday evening?" she continued.

"He said they were in all evening. Of course his girlfriend supported his alibi, but he did seem genuinely shocked at her death."

"They had been married eight years, so there must have been some sort of affection there. Did he say why they split?" she asked.

"He just said that they had drifted apart, although I got the impression that he would have said more if he had been by himself."

"According to forensic, Caroline Ryan wasn't sexually assaulted," Josephine stated.

"Well taking that into consideration, plus the fact that nothing was missing from her flat, I wonder if it could be some sort of personal vendetta," the sergeant suggested.

"I've got statements from her friends June Dwyer and Sheila Simms from the Divorced and Singles club," DC Sally Fletcher informed them. "They were both shocked, and couldn't shed any light on who could have done such a thing. Apparently Caroline Ryan did have a lot of friends there."

"I think perhaps I ought to visit the place," Josephine said.

"What for... professional or pleasure ma'am?" DS Hughes joked.

"Probably both," Josephine replied. "Anything else Fletcher?"

"Well yes. Apparently June Dwyer had given Caroline a lift home from work on Thursday evening. They arrived at the flat about six-fifteen according to her. She said she only stopped for about fifteen minutes, had a coffee and left."

"Any luck with the residents?" Josephine turned to DC Barnes.

"One of the residents, a Mr Jones said he saw a woman with long black hair leaving the block of flats at about eight-thirty and she seemed to be in a hurry."

"Where was he when he saw her?"

"Well he's got a ground floor flat. His lounge window faces the gardens at the front entrance and he sits there a lot and watches people come and go."

"Hasn't he got anything else better to do?" asked Sergeant Hughes.

"Well actually sir, he's got MS and is in a wheelchair. I think he looks out of his window not to be nosy but just to help pass the time. In fact I've got the description here." He got out his notebook and started to read. "About thirtyish, rather tall, long black hair, and wearing a blue suit."

"Did he notice if she had arrived in a car?"

"I think he just watched her walk out of the gardens and on to the road."

"She may have parked there."

"Well there's plenty of room for visitors' as well as residents' parking in the grounds... I wonder?"

"Do you think he's reliable?" Josephine asked

"Yes, although he's physically weak with the MS he's only in his forties: I should say he's quite alert".

"That's funny because June Dwyer, who works nearby, gave Caroline a lift home. She's got long black hair, although I wouldn't have said she was that tall. Anyway, she left at six thirty," DC Fletcher added.

"Maybe people appear taller to him because he's in a wheelchair".

"Oh Bill, really! What a thing to say," Josephine nudged him.

"But listen, aren't we getting a bit carried away here? I mean this woman with long black hair, there are fifty flats in that block, she could have been visiting any one of them, not necessarily Caroline Ryan's."

"OK Barnes, tomorrow you'll have to knock on every door to see if anyone had a visitor of that description."

"Can I take a PC with me ma'am?"

"No, sorry Barnes, it's a hard job, but as the saying goes, someone's got to do it".

Sergeant Bill Hughes stood up with some papers in his hand.

"I've had information from forensic, no luck with the car I'm afraid, but Caroline Ryan did have a fluffy dog and a panda at the bottom of her bed. They had fibres of pink fluff from her candlewick bedspread on them, so apparently they'd sat there for a while. The teddy bear, however, had no trace of fibre which would indicate that either it did not belong to her or was not kept on the bed. Then again, there's always the possibility that she could have bought it as a present."

"Well, since no-one's ever seen the bear before, I'm convinced it was left by the murderer," DC Barnes interjected.

Josephine reached over for a file on her desk.

"Well I'd better tell you what information I obtained from the forensic pathologist. The only stomach contents were a cheese sandwich, but she'd consumed a large quantity of red wine. I'd say at a guess that she had the sandwich at lunchtime as she was going to her mother's that evening for a meal. I suppose she could have gone to the pub in her lunch hour although it seems unlikely she would have that much to drink knowing she had to go back to work. Which brings us back to the theory that she knew the murderer and let the person in and they had a few drinks together."

"Well, since her car was out of commission I suppose she'd have got a taxi to her mother's house," Bill suggested.

"Let's get the flat checked for any empty bottles, and DC Fletcher..."

"Yes ma'am?"

"Talk to June Dwyer again. If it's true that she did

leave the flat at six-thirty, see if she can prove what time she arrived home, any witnesses, et cetera."

Just at that moment there was a knock on the door and PC Richards came in.

"Chief Inspector Cunningham wants a word with you in his office ma'am"

"Well at least I've got something to keep him happy for a while."

Chapter 5

"OH, HELLO MUM, you look tired."

"Do I?"

"Had a bad day?"

"No worse than usual I suppose." Josephine muttered. "Are you going to Sandra's, only I don't feel like cooking tea."

"Well actually I've asked a few friends round."

"Oh great, just when I felt like a quiet night! Did you have to Jessica?"

"Well, there are some pizzas in the freezer, so you won't have to cook them anything."

"No, but I'll have to listen to the music all night!"

"We'll go upstairs, then you can have the lounge to yourself."

"That's very kind of you, in my own house." Josephine kicked off her shoes and walked into the kitchen thinking *I suppose I'll just have soup and toast.* As she was sorting through some tins the phone rang.

"I'll get it, it's probably for me anyway." Jessica shouted down the hall.

"Oh hello Dad, how are you? Yes, would you believe it she's here... hang on, I'll get her."

Josephine took the phone.

"Tom, how are you? Oh, I'm fine, I'm just fixing myself a snack... Dinner? Well, I'm a bit of a mess to be taken out... eight-thirty? OK, it'll do me good I suppose: Jessica's got the clan descending upon us."

After replacing the phone she felt a little odd; they'd been married twenty years and he was asking her out on a date. At the same time she felt excited, like a young girl; a feeling she hadn't experienced for a long time. She made herself a cup of soup and took it into the bathroom to have a long soak. She slipped into the warm water. *This is just what my tired body needs*, she thought.

"This is a cosy place. How come we've never been here before?" Josephine asked as she looked out to sea.

Tom had taken her to a lovely little clifftop restaurant near Brixham, specialising in seafood. She picked up the menu and started to read it.

"Oh, I can see why we've never been here before, look at these prices."

"Never mind that. The chap at work said it was one of the best fish restaurants he'd been to; he highly recommends the Dover sole," Tom said.

Despite Josephine's reluctance, because of the prices, Tom still ordered it for her along with a bottle of white wine.

"That was delicious." Josephine finished her wine and sat back in the chair. She felt satisfied and content as one often does after consuming a good meal. Her eyes looked tired but she was relaxed.

"I must admit, despite the price, that was lovely." She reached over and touched Tom's hand.

"I wish it could always be like this," he replied as he squeezed her fingers.

"But life's not like that is it? That's why we're in this situation."

"I put a lot of thought and effort into this evening, I know I never used to in the past."

"Well, we all take people for granted, don't we? Especially those closest to us," she replied. "I know you felt neglected Tom, but I mean, I couldn't have given my job up. I've worked so hard to get where I am and financially we could never have managed, what with the mortgage and car loan, and you know how expensive Jessica's getting."

"Don't bring money into it again Jo."

"I'm not, but it's a factor."

"I mean, if you had just worked part-time," he suggested.

"The police force is a career and you can't work part time like a job in a corner shop." She became defensive.

"But it's taken you over Josephine; you don't seem to be able to detach yourself from the job."

"I know it seems like that at times, but you and Jessica are important to me."

"But maybe not enough."

"Oh, for God's sake Tom, I thought after such a nice evening we could have perhaps got things on a better footing. I was going to ask you to move back in."

"I'm not ready yet, there are a few DIY jobs that need doing to mum's house. You wouldn't believe the state she has got the place in since dad passed away. All the windows need locks; I mean, she is a pensioner living alone."

"You want to take a look at our house and never mind your mother's! I've been asking you to decorate the bedroom for ages," Josephine said angrily.

"Oh, so I can't help my own mother now? You know these workmen charge the earth and most of them are cowboys."

"Of course you've got to help her, I've always been fond of your mum, only God knows what she thinks of me now. I suppose you've been running me down to her."

"Oh for God's sake Jo, this is hopeless... I'll take you home."

"Don't bother I'll get a taxi."

"I asked you out and I'll take you home." He called the waiter over and paid the bill.

As they drove back in silence Josephine thought how hopeless the situation was. She looked over at Tom; he had made a real effort, with the restaurant and everything, yet they had still ended up arguing.

He pulled up outside their house in Babbacombe and looked up at Jessica's window.

"It looks like they're all still there. Do you want me to tell them to go home?"

"No it's all right Tom, I'll turf them out... look it was a lovely evening."

"Well, to start with it was," Tom replied.

She laid her head on his shoulder

"What's wrong with us Tom?"

"Well if I knew that, we wouldn't have a problem," he grinned. His smile always turned her on.

"Would you like to stay the night? It's been ages since we made love."

"Not tonight Jo... maybe when this lot aren't here," he pointed up to Jessica's room.

"You don't fancy me any more, do you?"

"Of course I do, I always have."

"Have you been to any of those Divorced and Single clubs?" Josephine asked.

"What a thing to say. Of course not! Have you?" he laughed.

"Not yet, but I'm considering it," she replied.

"Well, when you meet the man of your dreams, let me know, although he'd have to be a martyr to put up with your job."

Josephine got out of the car slamming the door. As she entered the house she shouted upstairs.

"Jessica, I want all your friends to go home now, I'm off to bed."

Jessica turned to her boyfriend.

"I think she's had another row with Dad, you'd all better go."

The following morning Josephine Blake felt quite perky and bright, despite the quarrel with Tom the night before. She'd enjoyed the evening; the fish meal had been light and hadn't lain heavily on her stomach, as the midnight snacks she consumed normally did. She'd got into a bad habit of eating late especially when she'd taken loads of paperwork home. The wine had relaxed her, and she'd slept well. At least she and Tom had talked. So they were getting somewhere, even though the evening had ended on a sour note.

She breezed into the office.

"Morning Bill… get them all in here will you?"

She pinned photos of Caroline Ryan's body on the board; there were several shots taken at different angles. She studied the one with the teddy bear. DC Barnes came in with DC Fletcher followed by Bill and two PCs.

"All take a seat, will you?" She turned to the board.

"Let's recap, Caroline Ryan, age thirty-six, strangled with

the tights, time of death approximately between eight and nine p.m. Now according to the forensic pathologist she wasn't sexually assaulted, and there was possibly a struggle, although no skin or blood was found under her fingernails. Nothing in the flat appears to be missing or disturbed, as far as we know and there was no break-in. Which points to what?"

She turned to DC Sally Fletcher questioningly.

"That she knew the murderer, or at least let them in herself ma'am."

"Right! We don't seem to have a motive at this moment in time. What do you think Sergeant?"

"Well ma'am, an attractive woman and yet no signs of sexual assault. Either someone had a grudge against her, or, if she let them in, it could have been someone she thought was selling something."

"Could money be a motive?" asked DC Barnes.

"Well, we've looked into her financial situation. She received eighteen thousand pounds from her divorce settlement, which she put down as a deposit on her flat. It's in quite an exclusive part of Torquay and would fetch about seventy thousand pounds. She had a mortgage for fifty thousand pounds attached to an endowment with a life cover and as far as we know her mother will inherit. She didn't have any antiques or expensive jewellery, although her flat was tastefully decorated. Then there's her car which is worth around one thousand five hundred," DC Blake informed them.

"She was still a regular at the Divorced and Singles club. I mean, could she have made an enemy there?" DC Fletcher asked.

"Good point! Hell hath no fury like a woman scorned,"

Sergeant Hughes interrupted.

"Unless she'd gone off with someone's husband or boyfriend which is highly unlikely as she'd been going out with David Vane," DC Barnes suggested.

"Mind you, I wonder who he was seeing before Caroline. He may have a jealous woman in his past," Josephine remarked.

She turned to PC Richards

"Now, any luck in tracing this woman with the long black hair who was seen leaving the flats?"

"Well ma'am it was a long job but we managed to speak to all the residents in Kew Gardens except two; the one's on holiday and the other's in hospital. The rest said they didn't have a visitor of that description."

"Do you think they were telling the truth?"

"As far as we could tell," the PC answered. "Why should they lie ma'am?"

"Well, there's a good chance ninety-nine per cent of the residents are telling the truth, but you never know. If one of them had a visitor who perhaps he didn't want his wife to know about, he might lie. So as to not to confuse matters let's assume for the moment that none of the residents knew this mysterious woman and she never visited any other flat. Therefore she must have visited Caroline Ryan."

"Now this friend June Dwyer who gave her a lift home fits the description to a T," the Sergeant said.

"Cast iron alibi I'm afraid, sir. According to her she left Caroline's flat at half past six and arrived back home at seven o'clock. She went out with her husband and some friends at eight o'clock to a restaurant. So there's no way she could have left Kew Gardens at half past eight," DC Barnes informed him.

"So, that lets her out, and yet it's funny the way the description fits. June Dwyer has long black hair; so does the woman seen leaving the flat. June Dwyer herself says she was wearing a blue suit and so was this woman. It seems rather an odd coincidence. The only difference we discovered is that June Dwyer is quite short, about five foot two. Even in heels she'd only be five foot four or five, and the witness said the woman was tall," Josephine said.

"According to June Dwyer she left her car, a red Mini, in a parking space right outside the entrance to the flats. But Jones said he saw the woman walk out of the grounds on to the road, so either she didn't have a car or she'd parked it elsewhere. Surely she'd have parked inside the grounds, unless she didn't want her car to be seen?"

"That's a good point Bill, I think we'll interview Mr Jones again. Now has anybody got any idea about this bloody teddy bear?"

"Let's say the murderer brought the teddy bear with them. Surely they'd want to get away from the scene of the crime quickly? To tie the bow around her neck so neatly and prop her up against the wardrobe with the teddy bear would have taken time. It seems as though they were setting a scene. This shows that the murderer was very cool and calm. They were taking the chance that no one else would call at the flat after they had killed her, so why not just get out as fast as they could," Sergeant Bill Hughes stated.

"Let's trace the make of the teddy bear and contact the manufacturers. They may be able to tell us who their wholesalers are, who in turn may have supplied local shops, although I suppose there are hundreds sold each week. I know it's a long shot, but we'll have to check it out." Josephine sounded unenthusiastic.

"The trouble is, we've got no motive up to now have we?" the Sergeant said.

"Well at least not one that we know of… nothing's missing, no sexual motive. I mean, it could have been the boyfriend; he called us, but you never know. Let's go and see this chap who lives in the ground floor flat and talk to him again. Ring him will you?" Josephine turned to DC Fletcher.

"Do you think it will do any good ma'am?" Bill said.

"Any better ideas?"

"Well no… not really."

"Then it's all we've got at the moment."

Chapter 6

"EXCUSE ME MISS, but these vegetables aren't warm."

"Oh I'm sorry. I'll get you some more." The waitress picked up the plate looking a little embarrassed. "Is everything else okay?" she asked.

"Yes, fine thanks."

"Any more drinks for anyone?"

"No, just the vegetables, unless of course you were going to offer me a free glass of wine as compensation," Karen Forbes suggested.

"I'll see what I can do." the waitress scurried away.

"My word, it's not like you to complain," Carol commented.

"Why shouldn't I? Twelve pounds a head. And they serve up cold vegetables." Karen replied.

"It's the new you, isn't it? You've become more aggressive since you've stood up to 'old man Myers'," Jan said teasingly.

"Well, more than stood up to him! He's not getting away with a thing." Karen said adamantly.

"What exactly was it you said to him?" Carol leant over her plate curiously as she sipped her wine.

"I made it quite clear I knew about his little fiddles, and that if he didn't do as I wanted, I'd make sure the management and his wife knew what he was up to," Karen replied.

"What exactly was he to do for you, a sexual favour?" Jan laughed nearly choking on her steak.

"Don't talk rubbish, I wouldn't touch him with a barge pole, he's not my type at all. No, what I'm after is more hours and a company car."

"Do you think he'd be able to arrange that? I didn't think he'd got that much pull in the company," Carol asked.

"Oh he'll do it all right. He'll have to, unless he wants to lose his wife and his job," Karen said as she finished off her wine. "Anyway let's not talk about it any more, I've had enough of work… Ah look, here's my vegetables and I do believe the waitress has a glass of wine in her other hand."

As she approached their table, a man got up hurriedly from the next alcove and barged into her, giving her arm such a jolt that she nearly lost her balance. Luckily she didn't drop the dish of vegetables, although the glass of wine went flying out of her hand. The man didn't apologise or even stop, but hurried out of the restaurant.

The waitress looked very upset, as if she would burst into tears at any moment. She placed the vegetables on the table.

"It doesn't seem to be my night," she said shakily. "I'll just go and get you some more wine."

"Typical bloody man. No manners," Karen said as she tucked into her meal.

Chapter 7

"**THANKS FOR SEEING** us so promptly Mr Jones. I'm Detective Inspector Blake and this is Detective Sergeant Hughes."

"That's okay, I've not got much to do these days." Mr Jones sounded depressed. "Shall we go into the lounge?" He turned his wheelchair round and they followed him in.

Mr Jones was in his forties, with red hair and a freckled complexion, but despite his illness he had a good colour.

"I believe you spoke to our DC Barnes a few days ago?"

"Yes that's right."

"We'd just like to go through a few details with you."

"That's fine," he replied.

"Now you say you saw a woman leaving at about eight-thirty?" Josephine asked.

"That's correct."

"Did you hear any noise that made you look outside for any reason?"

"Well as I told your constable, I was sitting by the lounge window. The days seem endless with this bloody thing." He looked down at his body pathetically.

"I often sit and watch people, I suppose I sound like a nosy old woman, but it just passes the time. I used to work all day and play squash in the evenings, go out for a drink with my mates and take my wife out until this… "

"Oh, I didn't realise there was a Mrs Jones," said DS Hughes.

"Well there isn't any more, she left. She'd stuck it as long as she could but what with losing my job, and of course as you get worse, your sex life ceases altogether."

"It must have been very difficult for you," Josephine said sympathetically.

"I get by." He sounded very sad.

"Anyway as you were saying Mr Jones..." Sergeant Hughes tried to get him back to his train of thought, unsuccessfully.

"Well, I was just saying, I was an active man. All I've got now is to look out and watch the world go by. That's why we picked a downstairs flat. We'd got a house, but as the bills started to mount up and the mortgage fell into arrears, even with my wife working we couldn't manage. So we sold up and moved here, the running costs are lower, and it's easier for me being on one level. I couldn't manage the stairs. We were lucky to get a ground floor flat and when it came on to the market we snapped it up. There was one for sale on the second floor which overlooked the gardens at the back, but at least here I see a bit of life."

"And you're sure of the time you saw this woman?" Sergeant Hughes asked.

"Yes I'd been watching a programme on TV which finished at eight o'clock. It was a fine night and I was going to sit at the back." He pointed to the patio doors that led out on to the grounds. "But I decided to sit in the window instead to see what was going on."

"Can you tell us again what you told DC Barnes? Take your time and think carefully," Josephine said.

"Well let's see, I'd been looking out for a while but nothing much was happening. You can see the road from here, and there's the entrance to the flats." They looked out of his window, to the left the entrance was about four yards away. He continued.

"Several people came in and out and also a woman who takes her dog for a walk at about the same time each night."

"I didn't think you could keep pets in these flats," DS Hughes remarked.

"Well in the contract it says you can keep a cat or a small dog, providing they're kept under control and don't mess the grounds, and aren't a nuisance to the other residents. The lady in question always takes her dog to the park over the road. Anyway not long after she'd gone I noticed this woman leaving. She seemed in a real hurry! She made her way to the road and as she turned the corner I heard a car engine start. I don't know whether it was hers or not."

"Now, can you give us a description again; as accurate as possible?"

"Well I don't think I can improve on what I've told you already. She was a tall woman with long black hair, wearing a blue suit."

"Was she carrying anything?" DS Hughes asked.

"I can't say I noticed. I suppose she must have had a handbag, all women do don't they?" he asked Josephine.

He suddenly felt a little awkward at what he'd said.

"I mean... I know you're a policewoman... "

"A Detective Inspector actually," Josephine informed him.

"Yes but you're still a woman. What I mean is, you have to put all your make-up and things somewhere." He felt uncomfortable. Josephine changed the subject.

"Now going back to her height: how tall would you say she was?"

"Oh about five foot ten or taller. She was wearing high heels."

"Are you sure about that?"

"Yes. She was in such a hurry and seemed a bit unsteady and wobbly as she walked."

"Mr Jones how tall would you say I was with my shoes on?" Josephine asked.

"Oh, about five foot six to five foot eight."

"And the Sergeant here?"

"About five foot ten, I'd say."

"Is there anything else you can think of?"

"I've racked my brain since I've spoken to your DC and I wish I could. I feel useless as it is," he sounded depressed and turned his wheelchair round and went down to the far end of the lounge.

"Please don't think that; you've been of great help and assistance," Josephine assured him, "here's my telephone number if you do think of anything else."

They thanked him and left.

As they got into the car DS Hughes said "Well he was quite close at guessing my height. I'm five foot eleven."

"I know, and I'm about five eight with my shoes on. I asked him because I did think he may have made a mistake about the height of the woman. I, like you Bill, assumed that as he was in a wheelchair and constantly looking up at people they'd have perhaps appeared to him to be taller than they actually were."

"Joan Dwyer's only short, about five feet two inches. Even in heels there's no way she could appear tall. So it must be sheer coincidence that she matched the description of our mystery woman," DS Hughes suggested.

"Well I suppose that's all we can assume at the moment, still if the woman is the murderer it at least ties up with there being no sexual interference."

"If this woman was only carrying a handbag at least she hadn't burgled the place! We didn't think anything was missing anyway, unless Caroline Ryan had some valuable jewellery, which could easily have been concealed. What do you think ma'am?"

"If it was a woman, it may have been act of revenge. Maybe they were both involved with the same man," Josephine replied.

"Where to now, back to the station?" DS Hughes said rubbing his eyes.

"Well I don't know about you Bill, but I've had enough for today. Drop me off if you like and you can go home and surprise your wife. We'll make an early start tomorrow."

He dropped Josephine home, as she hadn't taken her car to the station that morning. As he drove away from her house at Babbacombe he thought what a lovely sea view she had, and that if he'd have been given promotion, maybe he could have afforded a property like that. He was just about to take the route home, but changed his mind and went to the pub instead.

Chapter 8

"I DON'T KNOW ABOUT YOU but I'm so full I could burst."

"Well it's your own fault. You would have that second dessert," Carol giggled as she tottered along the marina.

"Well at least I'm not drunk. I've never seen anyone knock back so many brandies," Jan replied.

"I don't know what you two are moaning about. It was my treat," Karen said.

"And we do appreciate it don't we Carol?"

"Still, if we'd gone to a club we may have met some nice men." Carol started to sway and had to sit on a nearby bench.

"I feel a bit woozy," Carol said slowly.

"You're drunk. Come on, let's get you a taxi." Karen helped her off the bench with Jan holding her arm the other side.

"No I'm not, a little tipsy perhaps that's all… and anyway, I'd much rather have a decent meal and a drink than sex. I'm glad we never went to a club."

"We'll ask you that again when you're sober," Karen joked.

As the three women walked to the end there was a row of taxis waiting.

"Do you want to get a cab?" Karen asked them.

Jan looked at her watch.

"It's only eleven-twenty. The last bus to Paignton will be along any minute now; the ride might help Carol to sober up before she gets home to the old man."

"I'll pay" Karen offered.

"God you're flush; won the lottery?" Carol joked.

"Or maybe she's bleeding him dry at work… Oh look, here's the bus, it's early," Jan started to wave it down.

"Will you be all right Karen?"

"Yes fine. I'll get a bit of fresh air, and then I'll get a taxi home. Hurry up or you'll miss it."

She waved to them as the bus drove away. It was a lovely evening so she decided to walk past the pavilion and along the harbour to clear her head.

Chapter 9

CHIEF DETECTIVE INSPECTOR CUNNINGHAM was looking through the file on his desk.

"Well at least we've got that drugs case sewn up. A bit of good work there DI Blake."

"Thank you sir, but it's not over yet. I've got to appear in court next week to give evidence" she replied in a depressed voice.

"Think he might get off again?" the Chief asked.

"Oh! It's always a possibility, but according to his file and past history I should think he'd be going down for quite some time. I've checked everything thoroughly and I can't find any loopholes or technicalities that could get him off," Josephine stated.

"Well perhaps when that's out of the way you could put all your energy into this murder case," the Chief said a little sarcastically.

"We've been exploring several avenues sir, but the only thing we've got to go on is the elusive tall dark-haired woman seen leaving Kew Gardens."

"It's a nice spot there, and the surrounding houses are very smart, a bit of an up-market area, and you know how nervy people get when anything like this happens."

"Well I don't think there's a maniac going about sir, but it might be personal or domestic," Josephine informed him.

"Who have you got on the case at the moment?"

"DS Hughes, DC Barnes and DC Fletcher up to now sir."

"Well I might need Bill on another case if you can spare him."

"As I said sir, we've come to a halt at the moment in our

investigations, but if things pick up I shall need him."

"We'll discuss that if and when it happens."

"Okay sir. Anything else?"

"No, that's all, just keep me informed."

Josephine left the office and shut the door behind her. She walked down the corridor to her own department.

I should have stuck out to keep Bill on the case, even though I could manage without him at the moment, she thought to herself. She knew that when the Chief took someone off a case, you rarely got them back again. She felt angry and disappointed with herself for not standing up to him more.

As she entered her office, DC Fletcher said,

"That drugs case where you're giving evidence. Apparently the last lot of dope was bad and some user he supplied has died. The report's just come through and according to forensic he didn't OD, it was just bad drugs."

"Well it's a pity we can't add murder to his charge as well," Josephine replied. "I'll speak to our lawyer to see if it can be mentioned in court, although his brief will probably find some loophole so we may not be able to include it in the evidence."

Josephine sat down at her desk and looked through the file on Caroline Ryan.

"Get the boyfriend David Vane in. We'll interview him again to see if he can shed any light on this elusive woman with long black hair."

"Do you want to speak to him today ma'am?" DC Fletcher asked.

"No, tomorrow will do. I've had enough and I'm off home now."

Just as she was putting her jacket on the phone rang. It

was John Gardner the Forensic Pathologist

"Hello, I'm glad I've caught you."

"You're lucky I was just leaving." DI Blake replied.

"I just thought I'd let you know I've done a more thorough examination on Caroline Ryan. The strangulation was of such force that the windpipe was crushed. Normally only a man would have the strength to do that," he informed her.

"Well, women are stronger nowadays what with aerobics and weight training; that sort of thing," Josephine stated.

"I suppose you're right, but it's the strength in the hands that counts. Men's are larger and stronger than women's. I'm convinced only a man could do that sort of damage. Anyway I'll send you an official report."

"That's fine. Thanks for letting me know, John." She grabbed her bag and left the office.

Chapter 10

IT WAS ABOUT four o'clock in the afternoon when Josephine put her key in the door. There was a smell wafting through from the kitchen. Jessica was cooking beans on toast, and she'd got four plates laid out.

"Who's this for?" Josephine asked as she threw her bag onto the kitchen chair.

"Oh Mike's here with a couple of friends. I'm just doing us a snack."

"Are you going out afterwards?" Josephine asked wearily.

"I don't think so. We're all broke so we'll probably stay in and play some CD's."

"I really needed a quiet night Jessica, I'm so tired."

"We won't make a row. Will you tell them the food's ready?"

As they all came downstairs Josephine said

"You'll all have to take that up to Jessica's room to eat I've got a call to make."

"No problem Mrs Blake. You carry on with what you're doing and you won't know we're here," Mike smiled as he carried his plate upstairs.

I doubt that, Josephine thought. She kicked off her shoes and reached for the phone.

"Is that you Tom? I wasn't sure whether you'd be back from work."

"Yes I had to knock off early. How are you?" he enquired.

"Pretty drained at the moment. I was hoping for a quiet evening but Jessica's got some friends round."

"Say no more, I get the picture," Tom said.

"I was wondering, if you felt like going out for a drink, if you came over we could go to the Smuggler's Rest."

"That would have been lovely Jo, but I'm afraid I'm off to Plymouth for a couple of days."

"Oh that sounds nice." Josephine felt disappointed, but she tried to hide it.

"It's work actually. They want me to inspect some machines, and they've offered to put me up for the weekend, all expenses paid. Originally I offered to drive back and then I thought, why not if they're footing the bill."

"Oh well, I won't keep you." A note of anger crept into her voice. "Have a good time."

Tom detected the resentment.

"It's not a holiday, it's work. You should know all about that, the hours you put in. Anyway you're the one who is always saying I'm not getting on in my job so, I won't turn it down. This firm's a good customer and it might bring other work my way."

She realised Tom was right and that she was being unreasonable.

"You're right of course… Ignore me, I've just had a bad day and needed some company."

"Why don't you give Janet a ring? She'll cheer you up." Tom suggested. "As soon as I get back I'll ring you, see you later. Love you." He put the phone down.

I wonder if you do, she thought. She went into the front lounge and looked out. It was a lovely evening. She knew the only thing to do was go for a walk along the beach. She changed into her jeans, and trainers and went out.

As Josephine walked down the winding hill feeling

abandoned and lonely, she could see Oddicombe Beach ahead of her and smell the fresh salty air. She'd always had a feeling of tranquillity when the beach was deserted. It held a certain allure and enchantment. She walked along the shore, whenever she felt depressed and discouraged. It was very therapeutic, and today was no different. There was a slight breeze and the water lapped around the rocks. The sea shimmered in the sun. It looked lovely. After walking a little further she sat down and was absorbed by the view. As her mind became clear, she felt more sensible and realistic. Of course Tom had to concentrate on his career, hadn't she been telling him that for months? As for Jessica she didn't know anyone who had problem-free teenagers, and she herself felt lucky to be living by the sea. Seaside towns did have their fair share of problems, although not as many as the city where she used to live. At least by the sea you could escape for a while. If only in your mind.

She stood up, took a deep breath of air and felt as if a heavy weight had been lifted from her shoulders. *I'm alive and well, thank God*, she thought. *Poor Caroline Ryan won't see the sea again and you, Detective Inspector Blake, have got to find her killer; that's the one thing you can do for her.*

She walked back with a spring in her step. *I'll give Jan a ring and see if she wants to go out*, she thought. After a quick shower and change she cooked herself an omelette and salad, as the walk had given her an appetite. Just as she was about to pick up the phone it began to ring out.

"Hello ma'am, I hope I'm not disturbing you. This is DC Barnes here."

"Would it make any difference if you were? What is it anyway?"

"A woman's body has been found in a boat in the harbour at Torquay. The forensic pathologist, John Gardner, has been called, but we've been trying to contact you for ages."

"I'm sorry Barnes, I've been down on the beach. I should have taken my mobile with me and I doubt if anyone in this house would hear the phone. I'll be down as quick as I can."

DS Hughes was already at the scene.

"Hello ma'am, sorry to spoil your evening."

They walked along the path to the boat where the body had been found. As they went on board and walked to the end of the boat there lay a woman who appeared at first glance to be between the ages of thirty and forty. Her face and head were so badly beaten it was just a mass of red. Some of the blood was fresh and some had congealed; it looked a terrible sight. As Josephine stood there, her eyes transfixed on the victim's face, or what was left of it, John Gardner came up to her.

"So we meet again, Detective Inspector Blake."

"Unfortunately yes, but not in very pleasant circumstances. Do you think there is any link with the murder at Kew Gardens?" she asked.

"I wouldn't have thought so, I mean this one has been so badly beaten about the head, I'd imagine that the blows were so severe they were dealt with considerable force."

"So it was a frenzied attack do you think?"

"Definitely."

"And the weapon?" Josephine enquired.

"Hard to say at this stage. It could have been a hammer,

or a wrench; it was heavy whatever it was."

"And the time of death?" DS Hughes asked him.

John Gardner looked at his watch, it was seven o'clock in the evening.

"I'd say she's been dead about eighteen hours, so let's say a rough estimate of death would be approximately between midnight and two a.m. yesterday."

"No sign of a teddy bear?" DS Hughes joked.

"Well the boat's being searched by the forensic team and nothing has been found up to now."

"Caroline Ryan's death was far more tidy than this one, so this could possibly have been a drug-crazed lunatic, I suppose?" Josephine suggested.

"Well, it couldn't have been your man—could it ma'am? He's in custody at the moment isn't he?" DS Hughes remarked.

"Yes, but there's plenty more of them about."

Just at that moment DC Barnes came up to her.

"We've found her handbag on the pier ma'am. She's got some ID on her, her name's Karen Forbes and we've got an address for her in Paignton. We've also found a family photo and it appears that she's married and has two children."

"I think you had better go to her home then Barnes, and inform her husband what has happened. It may be a bit difficult, so take DC Fletcher with you."

"OK ma'am, I'll get on to it straight away." DC Barnes left the boat.

"Now, let's get back to this body Bill—she was found on the top deck so how come no-one noticed her earlier?"

"Apparently she had been covered with a sheet of tarpaulin that was on deck. It was fastened down so no-one knew there was a body underneath."

"Who's the owner of the boat?"

"He's a Mr Burns, he's waiting by the quayside. I told him we'd need to question him shortly."

"OK Bill, we'll go and have a word. Also could you arrange to have the harbour staff questioned to see if any of them can remember seeing anyone. Check with the owners of the other boats to see if they noticed anything suspicious, although to be honest I don't suppose many of them were about then."

They approached the man.

"Mr Burns, I'm Detective Inspector Blake and this is Detective Sergeant Hughes. I believe you're the owner of the boat?"

"Yes, that's right." He looked very pale and ill.

"Are you OK?"

"Well… yes… it's just that it was such a shock seeing all that blood over her face. I mean, I've seen a friend drown and that was terrible, but this…" He swayed a little.

"Let's have a seat." They went to a nearby bench on the promenade.

"I don't suppose you knew the victim? Not that you could see much of her face," DS Hughes asked.

"Goodness no, I mean it was such a shock."

"Do you keep your boat moored here permanently?"

"Yes, as you know it's very difficult to get a place at Torquay harbour."

"And how often do you use it?"

"Well mostly weekends I take her out, but some evenings, if it's fine like tonight, I'd go out for a sail."

"Do you know of any reason why the body should be

found on your boat?"

"No. I mean, as I said to you, I was getting it ready for the weekend to take the family out. Sometimes I bring my son down to help, although I'm glad he didn't come this evening."

"I'm sorry, you won't be able to use your boat until forensic have completed their work."

"Oh that's OK. I wouldn't feel right sailing her at the moment anyway."

"You've given your address and details to DC Barnes in case we need to contact you again?"

"Yes, that's right, if I can be of any help at all."

Josephine left DS Hughes talking to the man and boarded the boat. She wondered if the two murders could be connected. Even though the latest one appeared to be a violent and frenzied attack, the murderer had not been so out of control as to have left the body in full view. They'd been calm enough to ensure it was covered up to delay the discovery. Could it be the same person? Surely, two murders in the same area, a few days apart in a seaside resort…? She heard the sound of forensic zipping up the body bag and John Gardner came and stood behind her.

"You look daunted."

"Oh do I? I was just mulling a few things over in my mind. Bad for business this—two murders in just a few days: the Chief will be on my back."

"Well, I'll get back to the lab with the body straight away. We'll give this top priority—I'll do the report on my findings and get back to you immediately."

"Cheers John, I certainly need a result on this one." She went to the far end of the boat where the forensic team were working and DS Hughes came on board.

"There was no-one on duty at that time of night I suppose. The Princess Theatre would have been closed for at least two hours previously, so I don't think they'd have seen anyone about."

"We'll have to arrange to speak to her husband tomorrow."

"We could go today," DS Hughes suggested.

"No, I think that would be too soon, I don't think we should intrude yet—he'll probably be far too distressed to be of any help to us anyway."

"I'll get back to the station then." He looked around the harbour. "There are some classy boats here. I bet they cost a bob or two—I've heard the mooring costs are extortionate."

"It's out of our reach on a CID salary. The most we can hope for is a little rowing boat up the River Dart. Actually, thinking about it, I really like the Dart. Tom and I often used to hire a boat for the day. I find the river as relaxing as the sea, not that we've found the time to go lately. More's the pity. Anyway, come on, we've got work to do."

As they were leaving the boat one of the forensic team called out.

"Excuse me ma'am, I think you'd better come and look at this."

As she walked to the end of the boat the man was lying flat out, with his head right over the side of the boat looking into the water. As she approached he fished something out with a net which was dripping all over the deck, and there in the bottom lay a drenched and sodden teddy bear. Josephine turned to Bill; she looked solemn.

"Victim number two! I think we could have a serial killer on our hands."

Chapter 11

CHIEF INSPECTOR CUNNINGHAM walked into the incident room.

"There's no doubt that the two deaths are connected? I mean, you don't think a child could have dropped the bear in the water?" He turned to Josephine.

"That would be a very far-fetched coincidence sir. In my opinion they're definitely linked." Josephine sounded positive.

"If that's the case it looks bad for the Department. We've never had anything here like this before."

"Only those that Agatha Christie wrote about. What do you think she would have made of this one?" DS Hughes joked.

"This is no time for tomfoolery Sergeant. I suggest you lot get down to work on this case and I'll let you have some more reinforcements." He turned to Detective Inspector Blake. "I'd like to see you alone in my office in five minutes." He left the Incident Room abruptly.

Josephine turned to her team.

"Let's get a few things in motion. Barnes go and check on all the statements that the local bobbies have got from anyone on the harbour. Bill, go to forensic and see if they have unearthed anything, and Sally, get in touch with Mr Forbes and tell him we'll be paying him a visit. Get us a driver and we'll be off as soon as I've seen the Chief."

"Take a seat, this won't take long." The Chief sounded abrupt.

Oh God, that sounds ominous, Josephine thought.

"Do you think you can cope with this case?"

"Of course! I'm qualified and trained to deal with it."

"Yes, I appreciate that DI Blake, it's just that up until now you have dealt mainly with domestic murders and drug cases."

"And you think those are a piece of cake? Believe me sir, no case is uncomplicated or undemanding."

"I'm aware of that Detective Inspector Blake, I've been in the force a damn sight longer than you have. If it's a serial killer we're dealing with it will get nasty and perilous. Once the press are on it you'll have them all over you. If you have to give them a statement, play it down as much as you can. I understand you're having some domestic problems?"

Josephine was angry. She was infuriated by his last remark, as it was obvious someone had been gossiping. She was determined the Chief would not suppress her; she would not succumb to his hostility.

"My husband and I had some problems but it we've worked them out, and they've been resolved," she lied. "As for the murders, if they're linked to a serial killer, which we're not completely sure about, I do admit to not having dealt with one in my career. But perhaps with help from the psychologist we can try to ascertain how his or her mind works, which is more than can be said for the drug-crazed murderers. Finally sir, I know how awkward the Press can be. I've never been one to prattle on to them, I shall give them the facts and play the case down. I do appreciate that they tend to alarm and unnerve some readers with their articles." She stopped talking, feeling a little breathless and sweaty, although she felt he hadn't noticed.

"Well just let's say for the moment that you have convinced me that you can deal with this case, so don't let me down."

"I won't disappoint you," she said as she left his office. She'd never needed a cigarette more in her life and was tempted to get some from the canteen but curbed herself. *If I do start smoking again I'm damned sure it won't be because of the Chief*, she thought. Instead she settled for two cups of hot sweet tea and a doughnut and felt more composed.

DC Fletcher found her in the canteen.

"I wasn't sure where you were ma'am. I've contacted Mr Forbes. He's distressed, understandably, but you can go and see him now. DC James has a car available."

"Right, thanks Sally, I'll powder my nose and I'll be with you."

DS Hughes came into the canteen a bit excited and agitated.

"I've just been speaking with forensic and I thought I'd better let you know that a book of matches was found on the boat with a few spots of blood on them, and would you believe it—the matches were from the Blue Forest Club? Do you think they belonged to Karen Forbes?"

"Well, we don't know if she smoked. I suppose they could have belonged to friends and they ended up in her handbag—more to the point, they could have been dropped by the killer. That would tie in with Caroline Ryan's murder as she and her boyfriend, David Vane, were regulars at the club. We'll look into it later; we're just off to see Mr Forbes now Bill."

Josephine and DC Fletcher left the station.

Chapter 12

MR FORBES LIVED IN A BUNGALOW near to Paignton harbour. DC Fletcher rang the doorbell. A pretty girl of about nine years of age, with a mass of red curls, opened the door. Josephine realised at once that this must be the daughter, as she recalled Karen Forbes' bright red hair, mostly covered in blood. She suddenly felt quite sad as she looked down at the little girl and wondered how Jessica would have coped if she herself had died when Jessica was just a child.

"Hello there. Is your daddy in?" Mr Forbes came behind her in the hallway.

"Good afternoon Mr Forbes, I'm sorry to have to disturb you at such a time but we do need to speak to you. I'm Detective Inspector Blake and this is Detective Constable Fletcher." Josephine showed her warrant card.

"Oh—yes, I've been expecting you, come in. Would you like some tea or something?"

"No, that's OK sir, I'm sure you've got enough to do."

"Well my mother comes down each day to see to the children, but I'm afraid I've not been eating."

"Do you have another child?"

"Yes, I've a son Peter, he's fourteen. He's been going to his friend's mother after school. She's been very good; everyone has but it doesn't compensate."

"No, of course," Josephine said sympathetically.

"Can I go out and play Dad?" the little girl asked.

"Just go in the garden on the swing. Nanny will be here soon."

The little girl ran out of the back door.

"How's she coping?" DC Fletcher asked.

"I don't think it's sunk in yet; she seems to talk about her mother as though she's still here." His eyes welled up with tears.

"I know this is a bad time Mr Forbes, but we do have to try and find out who did this to your wife, and we need your help."

"Yes, of course."

"How did she happen to be out on Thursday night?"

"Well once a month she had a night out with her friends. They'd go and have a drink or sometimes a meal. I'll give you their names and addresses."

"Did your wife work?"

"Yes, she worked for a tourist firm by the harbour. When she first worked there they only used to organise things for holiday makers but now apparently the business has grown, and they do boat trips and business parties, executive conferences, all that sort of thing."

"Was it a full time job?"

"Yes. I didn't like her working full time, especially with the children, but we've only been in this house two years and we've quite a hefty mortgage, so her wages really helped out with the bills."

"So you never minded your wife going out?"

"Why should I? She worked hard, she deserved a night out with the girls. I go out sometimes with my mates to the local pub—we're in a quiz team. It's only fair that she should as well."

"Do you know if she ever went to a club called the Blue Forest?"

"Not that I know of, anyway that's a Divorced and Singles

81

club isn't it? A bachelor friend of mine goes there sometimes, so why should my wife go there? Why are you asking me about the place anyway?"

"It may be just a coincidence but a book of matches were found close to the scene of the murder and they came from the Blue Forest Club," Josephine informed him. "Do you know of anyone who would want to harm your wife in any way?"

"No one. I mean why should they? Surely you don't think she knew her murderer? I thought it was just some maniac."

"We don't know what to think at this moment Mr Forbes. Did your wife drive?"

"Yes, we have a car each, but she never took the car when she went out as she liked to have a drink. Actually her car was on its last legs and I'm sure it wouldn't have passed the next MOT—I was thinking of getting her another one, although she had mentioned a firm's car."

"Did your wife own a teddy bear?"

"No." He looked puzzled. "Why do you ask?"

"It's just that a teddy bear was discovered in the water near the place your wife was found."

"My daughter has some soft toys in her bedroom; I suppose she's got a teddy bear." Mr Forbes paused for a moment or two and a vacant look came across his face. "Do you think she suffered? I mean it must have been terrible for her…by herself. Why weren't her friends with her? Did she try to fight him off? I mean what was she thinking of at the end?" He sounded very distressed.

"I think she would have been unconscious after the first blow," Josephine tried to console him. "I believe that your wife was out with two friends that evening?"

"Yes, that's right. Jan and Carol."

"Perhaps we could have their addresses?"

"I've got their telephone numbers if that would help." He came back with a book. "Let's see." He flicked through the pages. "Yes, here we are, Jan Peters and Carol Brown." He provided the numbers.

"Thanks a lot Mr Forbes, that will be all for now," Josephine said as she stood up. "Rest assured we'll do all we can to find out who did this to your wife, and if you can think of anything at all which may help us, please ring me." She handed him a card.

"You can't bring her back though, can you? And you can't give my children their mother, or me a wife, even if you do catch them," he said, closing the door behind him.

The police car pulled up outside Jan Peters' bungalow, which was on the road leading to Cockington. As she answered the door she said

"Oh, hello, come in. I've been expecting you. Actually Carol's here, is that OK?"

"Yes, we can talk to you both together."

DI Blake went into the lounge followed by DC Fletcher. The two women seemed genuinely upset and distressed by the death of their friend.

"If only we hadn't caught that bus! What was she thinking of, walking around the harbour at that time of night?" Carol said tearfully.

"Well, I gather she'd lived here all her life and this isn't exactly a high crime area, so I suppose she felt reasonably safe. What I wanted to ask you was, did Karen ever go to the Blue Forest? It's a Divorced and Singles club." Josephine asked the women.

"Yes, I know. My sister goes there," Jan said. "But no, Karen's never been there; I'm sure she hasn't. We've never been, have we Carol?" Carol shook her head.

"Look ladies, are you sure of that? I mean, it would go no further. I do understand that married women do go there just for a social evening, not to meet anyone else. I'm married and I appreciate that you do get fed up with the old man sometimes." The two women warmed to Josephine.

"It's nice to meet a policewoman who is human."

"I'm a Detective Inspector actually," Josephine informed them.

"If we'd been there we'd tell you. We've nothing to hide, honestly. Although it sounds quite good to me—we'll have to try it sometime."

"Why are you asking us about this club? Has it anything to do with Karen's murder?"

"We don't know at this stage, it's just that Karen's death could be linked to another murder victim, Caroline Ryan of Kew Gardens. Apparently she was a member."

"Do you mind if I've a cigarette?"

"No. Please go ahead," Josephine answered.

Carol lit a cigarette and walked to the window of the room.

"I wish we could be of some help. I know Karen was a bit of a hard case at times, she liked to get ahead in life, but from what we can gather she was very happily married. She always said that she and her husband had a good sex life, and he always put his money on the table. I don't think she was interested in other men."

"Well then, can you think of anyone who would want her dead?"

"Was it deliberate then? We thought it was a mugger or a madman who had attacked her and that she was just in the wrong place at the wrong time."

"Well, we're treating it as a murder enquiry. Whether it was planned for a reason or as you say, just a senseless attack, we're not quite sure yet. Did she have any enemies?"

"Not that I know of. I mean, she was well liked at work, I suppose." Carol Brown sounded vague.

"Don't you agree Jan?" She looked at her friend for reassurance.

Josephine sensed the uncertainty immediately.

"Look, I know she was your friend and you're both understandably upset, and perhaps you feel it would be disloyal to say anything detrimental about her now that she's dead. But if you were really fond of her and genuine friends, you're not helping by withholding information. Anything you can give us, no matter how minor or trivial it may seem to you, if it helps us to find her killer then I'm sure she would have wanted us to know. She would want to be avenged and so would her husband and children."

Jan thought for a moment or two.

"Of course, you're right, it's probably nothing, but..." she turned to her friend, "Do you remember Carol, at that restaurant, the night before she died?"

Carol pondered.

"Oh yes, she was talking about her boss, Richard Myers. I think that's his name.

They still seemed reluctant to tell Josephine anything but eventually she got the story out of them. Apparently, according to Carol Brown, her boss was fiddling the firm to line his own pockets, and also cheating on his wife. It seems that Karen threatened to inform on him to his superiors unless he got her some extra work and a company car.

"Do you think he was in a position to be able to achieve that?" Josephine asked them.

"Well, I work at the same place but in a different department, Carol doesn't work there—I don't really know him. I suppose Karen must have thought he could get them for her, otherwise she wouldn't have threatened to expose him."

"So, in fact, we're talking about blackmail?"

"Oh, it sounds awful when you put it like that," Jan said.

"What sort of person was Karen? I'd like an honest opinion," DI Blake asked.

"Well, I mean this recent thing, it was a bit out of character. She was a reliable friend, although lately she did seem to be getting a bit pushy." Carol informed them.

"And a lot more career-minded I think," Jan added.

"At one time it was just a job to get extra money to pay the bills, but she became more interested and anxious to get on in the business."

"And getting this information on Richard Myers could have been the opportunity she was looking for?" Josephine suggested to them. "Incidentally, that evening you went out for a meal, did you happen to notice if Karen had a book of matches with her?" Josephine asked.

"Not that I know of. She didn't smoke."

"Thank you both, I'll be in touch." Josephine left with DC Fletcher. As she got into the car Josephine turned to DC Sally Fletcher.

"I think we'll go and see this Richard Myers now." She leant over and gave the driver the address of Karen Forbes' workplace.

"Do you want me to ring him on my mobile ma'am?" DC Fletcher asked.

"No, let's surprise him. I'll drop you off at the station and you can check the statements. DS Hughes can come with me if he's free."

Chapter 13

MR MYERS' SECRETARY asked if they had an appointment. Josephine showed her warrant card and said that they needed to speak to him urgently.

"Oh, yes of course." The secretary quickly left the office and came back after a few moments.

"Mr Myers will see you now." They went into his office.

"I'm Detective Inspector Josephine Blake, and this is Detective Sergeant Hughes. We're investigating the death of your working colleague Mrs Karen Forbes."

"Oh yes. Of course. I spoke to her husband on the phone. Poor chap, he sounded very cut up. It's a terrible business."

"How did you get on with Mrs Forbes?" DI Blake enquired.

"We had a good working relationship, I shall miss her."

"Really. I'd have thought that you might have been relieved."

"What do you mean?"

"We believe that Karen Forbes had some information concerning your honesty at work, and that she may have threatened to use it against you."

"News to me! Who's been feeding you this line?"

"I'm afraid we're unable to name our source of information Mr Myers."

"What criminal acts am I supposed to have committed?"

"We were hoping that you could tell us that."

"There's nothing to tell—if you suspect something you'll have to prove it."

"Are you having an extramarital affair, Mr Myers?"

"Well if I was—it's none of your bloody business. But if

you must know, I love my wife."

"Most men who have affairs do," suggested DS Hughes sarcastically.

"Well if you can't help us, perhaps your wife can," Josephine suggested.

"Leave my wife out of this."

"Well if you have nothing to hide… "

"Yes, but you know what you women are like. You get a bee in your bonnet and there's no changing your mind," he turned to DI Blake.

"We women, as you put it Mr Myers, are a damned sight more sensible and intelligent than you could possibly imagine. I'm investigating a murder, not having my sex criticised."

Whoops! thought DS Hughes, *he's hit a weak spot there, the feminist is coming out in her now.*

"All right, I've had the odd fling with one or two women."

"Did Karen Forbes know about this?"

"Well, she'd perhaps seen the odd thing and put two and two together. She had no proof though."

"Was she blackmailing you?"

"Certainly not! The idea is preposterous!"

"Could you tell us where you were last Thursday evening, say between eleven p.m. and two a.m.?"

"I went down to the local pub for a couple of drinks and got back at about ten-thirty I think."

"Can your wife verify the time?"

"I don't know, she was asleep when I got in."

How convenient thought Josephine.

"It was a very nasty sight you know. Her head was caved

in and there was blood everywhere. forensic managed to clean her up before her husband identified her. Of course, it's the children I feel sorry for."

The colour drained from Richard Myers' face.

"It sounds awful, and I'm sorry, but it was nothing to do with me. You've got to believe that."

"Have we? Well, we'll be in touch. Goodbye Mr Myers."

DC Barnes walked into the office.

"Do you suppose she was blackmailing him, ma'am?" he asked DI Blake.

"I don't know Barnes. I want you to look into his job to see what it entails. See if there's any way that he could embezzle money from the company. Check up if there's any small fiddles he could have been up to."

"Shall I go to the Managing Director?"

"Not just yet. Try and find out what you can from the rest of the staff first."

"OK ma'am I'll get on to it right away. Oh, by the way, here are the photos from the lab sarge."

Bill put them on the board next to Caroline Ryan's photo, stood back and lit a cigarette

"One nice clean cut murder, and one very messy bloody murder. The one link is the teddy bears, so obviously it's the same murderer. I think the murderer took the teddy bear to the first murder," Bill stated. "And in the second case, perhaps they threw the teddy bear on to the boat, missed and it landed in the water. We'll have to have a word with the police forensic psychologist to see if they can give us an insight into a murderer who's into teddy bears."

Just at that moment the phone rang and DS Hughes picked it up.

"Oh, yes, quite… I'll let her know… I think she'll want to go and see the Home Office Pathologist as well… OK, that's fine, thanks."

He put the phone down.

"Forensics found quite a lot of blood on the pier, and also hairs belonging to Karen Forbes. Apparently it ties up with what John Gardner, the forensic pathologist, came up with and he wants to see us."

They entered the path lab and donned caps and gowns.

"I hope you've got something good for us John, we're getting desperate," Josephine said.

"Well, it's not a lot to go on but the amount of blood we found on the pier suggests she may have been dead, or at least unconscious, and was either dragged or carried to the boat. Since there wasn't much blood leading down to the body, and only one or two drips on deck, I'd think it was more than likely that she was carried, possibly over the shoulder say, like a fireman's lift."

"Surely it would have taken a man's strength to have achieved that? So there goes our dark, mysterious woman suspect," Bill remarked.

"We also found some fibres on Karen's body that appear to have come from a tweed jacket," John Gardner informed them.

"Tweed material is popular for both men's and women's jackets nowadays, so that might not be much of a lead. Anything else?" Josephine asked.

He walked over to Karen Forbes' body, which lay on the table, and uncovered her.

"Well, as you can see, there are some bruises at the top of her arms. It's possible the murderer caused them as she was grabbed in the struggle. She also has a considerable amount of bruising on one thigh, caused by falling against something, or her leg could have been knocked whilst her body was being dragged or carried on to the boat. Apart from that, she was quite a healthy woman—all her organs were sound and she looked after her teeth. A little overweight, but that's about all I can tell you at the moment. By the way, I believe the forensic team have got something on those book matches for you."

"OK. Thanks. I'll nip into the path lab on my way out," Josephine said.

The path lab informed her that Karen Forbes' fingerprints weren't found on the matches, which reduced the possibility that they had belonged to her. This led Josephine to think that it was more than likely the murderer dropped the matches.

DC Barnes, DC Fletcher and DS Hughes were seated along with four other police officers who had been assigned to the case.

"These matches are the best clue that we have had so far. I think we can assume they belong to the murderer. Caroline Ryan was a regular at the Blue Forest club, so was her boyfriend and friends. As far as we know from Karen Forbes' husband and friends, she never went there, but we can't be sure of that."

"I was thinking Sarge, that if the murderer was a member of the club, he might have known Karen Forbes from there. What do you think?" DC Barnes asked.

"I'd say that that's more than likely," Bill replied.

"Well, you and Fletcher carry on investigations around the harbour—see if anyone has seen anything, check all the taxi firms as well and see if any of them have noticed anything unusual."

"Anybody good at accounts?" Josephine asked the team.

"I've got an 'A' Level in Maths," one PC said a little bashfully.

Josephine turned to Bill.

"I want you to try and get your hands on all the accounts of the tourist firm that Karen Forbes and Richard Myers worked for. Get the PC here to go through them to see if there is a possibility that he could have been fiddling the accounts. I'd have thought that if Karen Forbes was blackmailing him she must have had something definite to go on. Bill do you fancy a trip to the Blue Forest club?"

"Well, OK, as long as you don't tell the missus!"

Chapter 14

THE MANAGER'S ACCOMMODATION was a flat above the club, situated not far from Churston. DC Hughes rang the bell and the door was answered by a tall man with dark hair, aged about forty, wearing jeans and a flowered shirt. As soon as Josephine looked at his face, the feature that struck her most was that he had very defined eyebrows, unusual in a man but they looked quite attractive, she thought.

"Good afternoon. Mr Laurence Philby?"

"Yes, that's correct."

"I'm DS Hughes and this is Detective Inspector Blake. May we come in?"

"Oh yes, of course. Your station phoned to say you were coming. Do come up."

They followed him up the stairs to a very comfortable looking flat, with deep pile carpet, chandeliers and the very latest large screen television. Bill looked round in envy—he'd been after a television like this for ages only they were about three thousand pounds.

"Nice place you've got here. The divorced and singles business must be doing well," he said a little grudgingly.

"Oh thanks… yes, business is good at the moment, we have quite a few members. Mind you, it hasn't come easy. I try hard to keep high standards: we have a good bar staff and I make sure that the beers and lagers are good and I never sell cheap plonk."

"Well it's nice to hear you don't water the beer down!" Bill joked.

"My regulars wouldn't come back if I did and we have a

good disco, not too loud as most of the people we get in here are aged between thirty to sixty and the last thing they want to hear is that 'rap' rubbish."

"I couldn't agree more," Josephine added. "I hear it blasting out every time I get home... anyway let's get down to business. I don't know whether you have read about it in the newspapers recently, but a young woman was murdered, a Caroline Ryan. I believe she was a member here."

"I know, a dreadful business. Yes, Caroline has been coming here for about a year or so. I also know her boyfriend, David Vane. They met here actually."

"Do you know most of your members?" DS Hughes enquired.

"Well no; I mean we get about a hundred in each night we're open, but I do tend to know the regulars. Sometimes when people meet a partner here they stop coming but Caroline used to come for a night out even when they were together—they enjoyed the music."

"What's the position with the membership?" Josephine asked.

"Well people can come twice without joining, they just have to sign the book. Sometimes they don't come back again! You see we get a lot of married people here which we like to try and avoid because they don't mind a 'one night stand' but they don't want to get involved in a relationship. The majority of our members are divorced, single or separated and when they do join we ask for proof of their marital status before we issue them with a membership card. It's ten pounds a year to join."

"Are you really that strict with the rules? Only I know of

some married women who come here even though they're happy with their spouse, but just say the music is good."

"I suppose it's like anywhere. Some get through the net, or they may come once and then leave it for a few weeks and next time they visit they sign the register with a different name, but I'd like to think that the majority of our members are genuine."

"I believe you have your own book matches?" Josephine stated.

"Yes, I thought it would be a good advert for the place." Laurence Philby got up and walked over to a nearby cabinet and produced a book of matches; they were dark blue with a white tree as a motif. He handed them to Josephine; one side said Blue Forest Club and the reverse read The Ideal Venue for the Unattached showing the telephone number underneath.

"We just leave a couple of ashtrays of matches on the bar and some on each table... are they important? I mean I don't see your point."

"It's just that a book of your matches was found close to the scene of the crime," DS Hughes informed him.

"Are you referring to Caroline Ryan?"

"No, actually it was the second murder victim, Karen Forbes. We didn't find any when we searched Miss Ryan's flat."

"Although I believe neither she or David smoked," Mr Philby added.

"Yes, but I suppose sometimes people may take them as a memento of their visit, or just out of habit because they're free," Josephine suggested. "It could be that the matches belonged to Karen Forbes and she got them from your Club or they could have been dropped by the murderer. Then again, there may be no connection whatsoever. People often ask for a light and they could have been given by a Club member to almost anyone." She stood up and walked over to the window.

"It's just that Caroline Ryan was a member here so there could be some connection between the two murders."

"It would be helpful if we could look through your membership book," Sergeant Hughes suggested.

"Yes. Of course, it's in the office, I'll go and get it for you." He returned after several minutes with a red, leather-bound book. It looked like a ledger and was set out in columns, giving name and address of each member, their status—divorced, single, et cetera, and also their signature.

"Would you like me to make you some tea?"

"Yes thanks." DS Hughes nodded.

Laurence Philby disappeared into another room and later returned carrying a tray bearing two exquisite china cups and saucers, together with a plate of biscuits and placed it on the table. As Josephine was drinking her tea she commented on how pretty the china was, but that it wouldn't last five minutes in her house without being broken. Sergeant Hughes wished he'd been given a mug as a cup was never enough for him! He drank his tea rather quickly.

"Are these names and addresses genuine? I see you've got ID by the side of most of them."

"Yes, that's when we've seen proof of the member's status, but as I said, sometimes people come for one night only and they don't need an ID, it's only after their second visit we ask them to join. From time to time we organise the odd trip or meal out for members to get together."

"And the Club itself—what nights do you open?" Josephine asked.

"Tuesdays, Saturdays and Sundays," he replied.

"You've never thought of opening every night?"

"People just haven't got the money to come all the time," Philby informed them.

"I'd imagine most of them work full-time," the Sergeant remarked.

"Yes, but we do have a lot of lonely people here hoping to meet someone. In the week they probably don't get home from work until late and are quite content to stay in and watch TV. It's just that, apart from those who have children and perhaps see them at the weekend, other members find that Saturday and Sunday can be a long day and they look forward to going out in the evening. Apart from which there's always more money about at the weekend."

"But you must get married men and women just looking for a bit of excitement?" Sergeant Hughes smirked.

"Of course we do, but they only come once or twice if they're not members."

"Do you mingle with your members?" Josephine enquired.

"Yes, I'm in the club most of the time, I've two ladies on the door who take the money, which is four pounds for non-members and two pounds-fifty for members. Occasionally I serve behind the bar if we're short-staffed, but usually I walk round the club and chat to people. Sometimes I'll announce a birthday or engagement over the microphone and I've even stood in when my DJ's been off sick. I like to get involved."

"Do you know of anyone who may have wanted Caroline Ryan dead?" Josephine asked.

He sat down and looked a little shocked.

"No, I don't—I mean, she dated a lot of men from here, but I don't think she clicked with anyone until she met David."

"I believe they argued a lot," Josephine suggested.

"I've seen them have a few words from time to time, but if relationships were perfect I'd be out of business!"

"Yes, I suppose you would," Josephine agreed.

"Do you ever have any trouble here?" DS Hughes asked.

"We've had the occasional fight. And once we had three or four young men come in, presumably holidaymakers, who caused trouble. I've stopped that now by not allowing groups of more than two youths in. Normally our members are aged between thirty and sixty and are quite respectable. Mind you, I've had the odd woman get drunk and throw a tantrum, especially if she's seen a man she was keen on, or perhaps had a date with, getting off with another woman. Women can be so bitchy at times."

DS Hughes smiled to himself. *You haven't got to work with this one!* he thought. *I wonder how she'll take that remark.*

Laurence Philby suddenly realised what he'd said as he looked over at DI Blake and smiling weakly, blustered "Present company excepted."

"Don't you believe it! I can be a real bitch—can't I Sergeant?"

DS Hughes kept his thoughts to himself.

"If I was too soft I wouldn't be a Detective Inspector, but at the same time I'd like to think I'm rather more sympathetic and compassionate than my male colleagues. Some things can be achieved just as well with tact and persuasion as with aggression." She smiled, rather sarcastically at both of them, and carried on looking at the members' book.

"We'll have to take this to the station and check it more thoroughly. Do you have a copy?"

"No, but that should be OK. We can start a new book to sign members in and I do have a record of the annual subscriptions."

"The Sergeant will give you a receipt and we won't keep it longer than necessary. By the way Mr Philby, are you married?"

"No, actually I've had a couple of long running relationships, and I lived with one woman for eight years, but never got around to tying the knot."

A bloke with some sense! Bill Hughes thought to himself.

"And are you seeing anyone at the moment?" Josephine asked.

He looked a little put out and annoyed.

"Well, I don't think it's any of your business. Surely it's not relevant to your enquiries?" He hesitated for a moment or two. "You do hear some rather sad stories from people about relationships and marriages which have gone wrong, especially when there are children involved. I personally prefer to stay single."

Although neither of them said anything, they both secretly agreed with him. Bill Hughes hardly saw his wife nowadays—what with the job and everything—and when he did have some spare time he spent it with his work mates drinking. This was better than being with a nagging wife. Josephine thought of the problems she was having with Jessica and the uncertainty as to how things would turn out between herself and Tom. Yet she still thought that was preferable to being alone.

They thanked Philby for his assistance and departed.

As they were driving back to the Station DS Hughes said, "Do you think he's gay, ma'am?"

"For God's sake Bill, any bloke who doesn't fit in with your idea of a beer-swilling, football fanatic… anyway he's had women in the past, although he could be bisexual."

"I mean look at those china cups, and the flat was decorated a bit feminine for my liking," Bill said trying to justify his previous remark.

"Not all single men live in a bedsit with a few cracked mugs, a chair and a bed, Bill!" Josephine said scornfully. "Tom often comes with me to choose furniture and pictures: he's got quite good taste. Anyway Philby lied about not having a woman in his life; the bedroom door was slightly open and I noticed some tights and pants on the bed—so obviously he's seeing someone."

"Then why do you think he said he wasn't?" Bill asked.

"Well, she could be married or one of his staff. He probably just wants to keep it under wraps… anyway fancy a spot of lunch?"

"Back at the canteen?"

"No, let's stop at the Smuggler's Rest, my treat. I've got the mobile if the station needs to contact us."

"OK ma'am, that sounds great." He wondered what he'd done to deserve this.

They sat in the Smuggler's Rest, overlooking the sea and tucked into homemade steak and kidney pie with ale. Bill had a pint of lager even though he was on duty but Josephine insisted he could only have the one and she ordered an orange juice.

"This is a lovely pub to have on the doorstep. I bet you come here a lot."

"We used to when we first moved into the house at Babbacombe, but we haven't been here for a while. You know Bill, I hope you don't think I'm interfering but you ought to take Mary out more, even though you work long hours."

Bill looked a little guilty.

"It's a vicious circle, I suppose, but I'm out a lot and when I do get home, Mary nags that she hasn't seen me and that we don't have a social life. So we end up rowing and I go back out again."

"I know it's difficult. We've got into the same situation but you must make the effort to take her out, otherwise you'll end up like me and Tom."

"I thought things were OK between you now?"

"Well, we may get it sorted, but I'm not sure. By the way Bill, I don't know if it was you who told the Chief about my marriage problems, but you probably know who it was even if you're not the guilty party. I don't want my private life discussed at work, understood?"

"Yes ma'am," he said meekly. "Would you like another drink?"

"No, we'd better be off now." Just at that moment her mobile phone rang. She stood up and went outside to get a better reception. "Oh! Right, he's in a bad way then? We'll get over there right away… yes, I've got the address." She pushed the aerial sharply back.

"The station's had a call from Mr Forbes; he's very distressed."

"It's Karen Forbes' funeral today, isn't it?" he asked. "I suppose that's why."

"It sounds even more serious than that."

DS Hughes went to get behind the wheel of the car.

"I'll drive Bill. I know you've only had one, but still…"

Chapter 15

KAREN FORBES' MOTHER-IN-LAW opened the door.

"Oh, that was quick… do come in, my son is very distressed." She led them into the lounge.

As they looked around they could see a buffet had been laid, and a nearby trolley contained drinks. The shelf was covered in sympathy cards.

"We're sorry to have to intrude on this occasion Mr Forbes, but I believe you telephoned the station."

"Yes, it was an early funeral and most of Karen's family and friends have left."

"How were the children?" Josephine asked. "Did you let them attend?"

"Yes, they wanted to—but I wish they hadn't now. They've gone to a neighbour's house. It was dreadful, just dreadful." Mr Forbes began to shake.

"I think you'd better have a drink son." Mrs Forbes brought over a large glass of brandy and carefully placed it into his trembling hands.

"Can I get you anything?" she asked Josephine and Bill.

"Coffee would be nice, thank you," Josephine replied.

Mrs Forbes left them and went into the kitchen. After several minutes and a few gulps of brandy Mr Forbes seemed more composed.

"I'm sorry about that," he said. "I'll be all right to talk now."

"Take your time," DI Blake said. "There's no rush." DS Hughes got out his note pad and pen.

"Well everything was fine. We'd arrived at the cemetery,

the vicar held a lovely service in the chapel and we went to the graveside. The children seemed to be holding up very well and I was trying to be strong for their sake, although inside… " His eyes welled up with tears and he appeared unable to carry on.

Josephine touched his hand.

"I understand what an ordeal it must have been for you." she said sympathetically.

"As we were leaving the graveside the children were either side and I was holding their hands so tightly, almost as if I was going to lose them as well, when Katie said 'Look Daddy, who's sent Mummy that? Can I take him home with me? He's lovely.' I didn't know what she was talking about and just squeezed her hand and said 'Be quiet darling.' She loosened my grip and ran over to the other side of the grave. 'Look here it is.' I looked over and amongst all the wreaths and flowers stood a teddy bear made from yellow flowers— roses, I think, but I'm not sure. I went over thinking how thoughtless someone had been. I mean you only send things like that to children's funerals, not adults', and of course you were saying how a teddy bear had been left nearby to where Karen was killed. I walked over and there was a blank card attached to the teddy bear wreath. How sick! Who could have done such a thing?"

Josephine looked over at DS Hughes—their thoughts in unison—could it be the murderer?

"Could you give me the name of the cemetery?" Josephine asked.

"Yes, it's Lye near to Dartmouth," he answered.

She contacted the station on her phone.

"Hello this is DI Blake here. Can you send DC Barnes or

Fletcher or whoever's available to Lye cemetery to inspect the grave of Karen Forbes… hang on a moment I'll just get the position for you."

Mr Forbes explained to them exactly where the grave was situated and she passed the information on.

"OK, have you got all that? DS Hughes and myself will join you there as soon as possible."

"Did you touch the teddy bear wreath at all Mr Forbes?" Bill asked.

"No, I was so horrified I just left, I can't imagine how anyone could have been so tactless." He looked at Josephine's face. It was stern and serious. "It's him, it's the murderer isn't it?" His voice became angry.

"It's a possibility. Well him or her, we don't know who the murderer is at the moment, but rest assured Mr Forbes we'll do everything in our power to catch them. I'm sorry such a terrible thing could have happened today of all days. Even your mourning and grief has been intruded upon. We shan't keep you any longer."

As they were leaving DS Hughes who rarely showed emotion of any description stopped in the doorway and patted Mr Forbes on the shoulder

"Don't worry old chap, they won't get away with this."

When they were back in the car he turned to Josephine

"What a bastard! I mean, even at the funeral! I don't suppose there's any doubt it's the murderer?"

"Well either that or they've got some very sick relatives or friends. Let's just hope it's still there."

As they reached Karen Forbes' grave it was covered with

beautiful crosses and wreaths, all with messages of sympathy and notes of affection attached to them. There standing high above them all stood a wreath in the shape of a teddy bear. It looked almost God-like and consisted of yellow roses and freesias and attached to its side was a 'Deepest Sympathy' card, with no writing on. Josephine turned to DC Fletcher.

"Right Sally, I want every single florists' shop contacted in the area. Check on everyone to see if anybody's ordered a teddy bear wreath in the last week or so. Get help from any PC that's available; I want no stone unturned. We also need to establish if it was brought to the grave by hand or delivered here."

"OK ma'am, I'll get on to it right away.

DC Sally Fletcher hurried away to a waiting police car.

"Now Barnes, question all the people in the chapel, and also any cemetery staff to see if anyone noticed anybody carrying a teddy bear wreath, or acting suspicious. Bill, I'd like you to get back on to Mr Forbes as we need a list of guests who attended the funeral. Any idea how much extra man-power has been assigned to this case?"

"I think we'll get another DC and possibly two PCs, from what the Chief said."

"Right then, I think we'll need all the guests questioned. I doubt very much that any of them are responsible but they may have seen someone leave it there. See if you can get help to handle that. I suppose it would be an idea to get David Vane and Caroline Ryan's mother interviewed to see if they can remember anything amiss at her funeral. I'll try and get to see the forensic psychologist as soon as I can. We've got to find out how the mind of this killer works, before any more murders occur."

Chapter 16

JOSEPHINE THREW HER CAR KEYS on the table and flopped into the chair. She felt absolutely exhausted, her body ached, and her mind was confused. One factor that may have contributed to this was that she hadn't had a proper meal since the previous evening. She thought that the house was unusually quiet and she relished the peace. Closing her she eyes dozed off for about fifteen minutes. On waking she remembered there was some white wine left in the fridge and poured herself a glass, grateful that Jessica or one of her friends hadn't demolished it. Feeling suddenly ravenous she opened the freezer and found a ready-made meal of chicken and pasta. *That'll do nicely* she thought reaching for the box. *Ten minutes on high power in the microwave. Thank goodness for convenience foods.*

As she took her wine into the lounge she noticed a note on the fireplace it read:

"DEAR MUM, GONE TO MIKE'S WE MIGHT GO OUT TO A CLUB, I'LL PROBABLY STAY THE NIGHT AT HIS PLACE. LOVE YOU PS BORROWED £10 OUT OF THE JAR HOPE YOU DON'T MIND"

"Well it wouldn't make any difference if I did," Josephine said out loud. As she was eating her meal she thought it was worth ten pounds to have the house free for the evening. Although it would have been nice to have had Tom here, perhaps she was better alone as she had a lot to sort out in her mind. This murderer was a force to be reckoned with and yet apart from Karen Forbes' boss, Richard Myers, they hadn't really got a suspect. She was desperate to get things moving. There were seven on the team now including herself and Sergeant Hughes, so the manpower was there but if she didn't get a result the Chief would be on her back again. She decided on an early night as she hadn't been sleeping well lately. It had crossed her mind, it could either be the menopause, pressure from the case, or just not having Tom next to her in bed. Not that they cuddled very often; he'd just roll over and snore most nights. Laughing to herself she remembered how she'd poke him in the back to shut him up, especially when he'd had a drink or two.

Yawning she felt she'd definitely sleep that night. As she was going upstairs the phone rang.

Oh damn, who the hell's that? she thought. She picked up the phone.

"Oh hello Tom, I was just thinking of you."

"Really? Nice sexy thoughts?"

"No, actually I was just remembering your snoring," she joked.

"Charming! Is that the only memory you have of me? Anyway I don't snore as loudly as you make out."

"Don't you? I'll have to tape you sometime." She paused. "That's if we ever sleep together again."

"Well that's why I called you actually, I've got a bottle and was going to come over."

"I was just going to bed."

"That's fine by me."

"I'm sorry Tom but I'm so tired. This case is really getting to me. There's been another murder and I'm not sleeping."

"You're sexually frustrated," he joked.

"No I'm not!"

"Oh, getting it elsewhere are you?"

"For God's sake Tom don't talk rubbish. Where would I find the time?"

"That's why we split up, because your job was taking over. If you cut it down a bit, we could at least try and work at our marriage."

"I will Tom, it's just this case. Whoever it is, they're a sick bastard. I mean two murders only days apart! I mean Torquay's not even a high crime area. No, I think we're dealing with some sort of maniac."

"Well for God's sake Jo be careful."

"I will. Look Tom, I'm sorry about tonight. I'll phone… love you." He put down the receiver and she didn't think he'd heard her last few words.

Josephine Blake slept well and the next morning she woke refreshed due to the fact that Jessica had not returned so there wasn't the noise and clatter of her coming in and making herself something to eat at an unearthly hour.

As she looked out of the window she saw it was a glorious day, there wasn't a cloud in the sky and a warm breeze wafted through. She didn't feel like going into the station, but like getting a good book, a bottle of wine, a comfy deck chair and spending the day on the beach *That's the disadvantage of living by the sea, on days like today* she thought.

As she applied her make-up and sipped coffee her thoughts went back to the day before, when she'd seen Roger Forbes so devastated. She felt anger welling up inside her thinking of what a sick act it had been to send that thing to the funeral. She felt sure it must have been the murderer unless the Forbes family had an enemy. Forgetting about an idyllic day on the beach she headed for the station.

On arrival she asked DS Hughes to get everyone assembled in the incident room. On the board there were now photos of both victims; Caroline Ryan's body propped upright with the tights around her neck and Karen Forbes' photo looking far more gruesome and bloody. They all sat down and Josephine took a gulp of coffee. For some strange reason she fancied a cigarette, but settled for chewing gum instead. She stood up and walked over to the board.

"Now if we can just re-cap for a moment as we don't appear to be going in any direction with these two crimes. Now, victim number one," she pointed to Caroline Ryan's photograph.

"No obvious suspect at this time. There's the boyfriend David Vane; he seemed genuinely upset but who knows. What motive would he have? The only person to benefit financially is her mother. No signs of a break-in, so let's say we're looking for a serial killer. Now the teddy bear; anyone got views on that?"

"Well he must have taken it with him. I don't suppose it's the sort of thing people normally carry about with them, and it didn't belong to Caroline as far as we know, so from that I'd say it was a carefully planned premeditated murder," DS Hughes stated.

The others nodded in agreement.

Josephine continued "OK, fine... now there's this mysterious tall dark woman seen leaving Kew Gardens by the tenant in one of the ground floor flats. She doesn't seem to have been known by any other resident so it's possible she's also a suspect." She turned to DC Roger Barnes.

"No, sorry ma'am. We've checked thoroughly; her description doesn't tie up with anyone except June Dwyer who gave her a lift home that evening. She seems very elusive, we can't trace her at all."

"All right let's assume she could possibly be the murderer, so we could have a female suspect. Now the second victim. A totally different murder, a frenzied attack: the head struck with such force that there was severe brain haemorrhaging according to the forensic pathologist," Josephine said.

"Caroline Ryan's windpipe was crushed which required a certain amount of strength, and the blows to Karen Forbes, also were dealt with force. I'm still convinced it's a man," Bill commented as he lit a cigarette.

"First impressions were that the two murders were not connected until the second bear was found in the water, but we do have a suspect of sorts, Richard Myers. Supposedly Karen Forbes was blackmailing him, not for money but certain things she wanted from him concerning her job. What did you get on him?" Josephine asked DC Barnes.

"We haven't got anything definite, although he doesn't always put the correct numbers of guests on trips and conferences; I should think he could put a false number down and make some extra cash, but I wouldn't say it was big money. I made discreet enquiries about his financial position. His basic wage is only about two hundred pounds per week, although he does earn commission on any bookings he gets. He has a daughter at University, and he sends her money and although he has a firm's car, his wife has a new car and she doesn't work. He has a detached house by Meadfoot Beach, and I'd say he seems to be living above his means, but we've got no definite proof," DC Barnes informed them all.

"There's always the possibility he inherited money from a parent or relative, or has savings which could account for him having that lifestyle," DS Hughes suggested.

"Yes Bill that's quite feasible. Now, what about this other thing Karen Forbes had got on him about his private life?"

"Well actually I've found something interesting," DC Sally Fletcher said proudly. She walked to the desk and turned the pages of the large red leather membership book from the Blue Forest Club.

"Here it is: Richard Myers. He's a member there, only he's written a different address down."

"I suppose that's because he wouldn't want any correspondence sent to his home," Josephine said.

"Have we got all these pages photocopied?" she asked Bill.

"Yes they're all on file. I suppose we can return the book to Philby now."

"The information Karen Forbes had about his private life was probably correct. If he was a regular at the club, he could easily have had some book matches. I think we'll have to interview him again. It also might be an idea to ask Mr Forbes if Karen had ever mentioned anything to him about her boss, although she probably wouldn't have wanted her husband to know she was blackmailing him. The poor chap is so distressed at the moment with the teddy bear wreath being left at the grave... any views on that, apart from the obvious... that's he's a sick bastard?"

Bill stood up and walked round the desk.

"When we interviewed Myers, I wondered if he realised he was a suspect; only if he did surely he wouldn't have risked leaving anything at the grave in case he was recognised," he said thoughtfully.

"I'm of the opinion that the murderer thinks it's a sort of game, but he's taken it a bit too far to send something like that to a funeral. If he can't let the dead rest in peace, surely he must have realised the distress it would bring to her family, as if he hadn't done enough depriving them of a mother and wife," Josephine said with a sigh.

"Any luck with the florist shops?" Bill asked DC Fletcher.

"We've visited shops in Torquay, Paignton, and Teignmouth so far. All the teddy bear wreaths ordered were checked, and they were for children's funerals, including one cot death. It was a rather depressing task actually and we've got a lot more to visit yet," she replied sighing.

"1 suppose whoever ordered it would have paid cash so it couldn't be traced... Now on a lighter note... " Josephine was feeling quite melancholy and wanted to change the subject.

"Does anyone feel like tripping the light fantastic?" she asked the team. They all looked a little confused.

"What do you mean ma'am?" Sally Fletcher asked.

"Oh, of course. You lot probably wouldn't have heard of that expression... I'm showing my age again! What I was trying to say was does anyone fancy a visit to the Blue Forest Club undercover to see what they can find out?"

The two PCs and Barnes seemed rather keen but Josephine plumped for DC Fletcher.

"I think people tend to open up more to a woman; you know how women gossip in the loo when they're putting their face on. How old are you Sally?"

"I'm thirty-two ma'am."

"I don't suppose that's too young, you'll fit in nicely. I'll brief you later about the procedure."

Just as Josephine was leaving the room she said,

"Oh by the way take a friend, it may look odd going alone."

After she'd left the room DS Bill Hughes turned to Sally.

"You lucky sod! Socialising in work's time."

"What's the boyfriend going to say, that's what I'd like to know," Roger Barnes said teasingly.

"I'm amazed the DI's not going herself. I hear she's not getting on with her old man," one PC remarked.

"Well, the owner Laurence Philby, has seen us both. If Sally goes it won't look suspicious," DS Hughes informed him.

Chapter 17

THE SECRETARY showed Detective Inspector Josephine Blake into the room, which looked clinical and yet plush at the same time. The carpet was powder blue and the furniture black ash, it looked very ordered and impersonal.

"Doctor Andrew Blythe won't keep you waiting long. He's just finishing a lecture. Can I get you something while you're waiting?"

"Yes, please tea," Josephine smiled.

Some twenty minutes and two cups of tea later she was still waiting for the forensic psychologist, although funnily enough she didn't feel impatient or restless. It wasn't often she had any time to herself to sort out her mind. She wondered if a psychologist could solve the problems she and Tom were having. Not that there was a problem really, just a case of getting back on the right footing again. *Still, I'm here to ask for help with this serial killer,* she thought to herself. If it was a serial killer, this modern-day word that seemed so popular in books and television. It was almost as if one murder wasn't enough nowadays to attract the viewer's attention.

She felt the teapot with the intention of pouring herself another cup, but it was cold. Just at that moment the door opened and a rather attractive looking man entered. He was in his forties, with mousy hair flecked with grey.

"I'm so sorry I kept you waiting… Detective… er," he couldn't remember her name.

"Detective Inspector Blake," she informed him.

"Oh yes, of course, my secretary did tell me earlier."

He placed a large folder on the desk.

"Oh I see Judith's been looking after you," he said noticing the tea tray. "Would you like some more?"

"No thanks, I've finished the pot as it is."

He pressed his buzzer and the secretary entered.

"Could you make some more tea, just for one please?"

She picked up the tray and left the room. As he sat by the light of the window Josephine noticed how striking his eyes were, a pale icy blue. They were attractive but at the same time stern and unfriendly. She studied his face, he had a lovely smile yet his eyes were cold and unresponsive.

He sat back in his chair and put his hands behind his head.

"Are you scrutinising my face Detective Inspector?" he asked a little sarcastically.

"Oh... no... I mean... " Much to her annoyance Josephine flushed.

Dr Andrew Blythe smiled.

"I didn't mean to embarrass you. I do have a knack of knowing what people are thinking. It's my eyes isn't it?"

Josephine answered bluntly and then wished she hadn't.

"They don't seem to fit your face. They appear clinical, if you don't mind me being candid."

"That's what my ex-wife used to say. My father was Norwegian and I've inherited his eyes I'm afraid. Although they can be an advantage sometimes. People seem to think I'm being serious and studying them, even when I'm not."

Josephine liked his forthrightness. It was a quality she'd always admired, as she couldn't stand people who were vague. She'd had problems with Tom and people she worked with when they avoided giving her a straight answer and sidestepped the issue. She suddenly felt a certain warmth towards the man sitting opposite her, which she thought was unprofessional of her as she'd come to consult and liaise with him in the hope of solving the case. *It must be my hormones, I seem emotional*, she thought putting herself in check.

"Now if we can get on Dr Blythe," she said.

"Call me Andrew and may I call you…?"

"Josephine," she answered reluctantly.

"Well, I've got some notes on the crimes to date, though I feel it always helps to be at the scene to get a better idea. Now the first murder." He leafed through some papers till he found the one he wanted.

"I've a photo here." Josephine handed him the picture of Caroline Ryan's body sitting upright, with the tights tied at the side of her neck and the teddy bear next to her. Afterwards she showed him Karen Forbes' body with the head and face badly disfigured.

"And you say she was the second victim, this savage and frenzied attack?" he asked Josephine.

"Yes that's right Karen Forbes was murdered several days later."

"I find this odd," he said thoughtfully.

"Originally we didn't think the two murders were linked as they were so different. It wasn't until the second bear was found in the water… " Josephine added "I mean we're looking for a serial killer aren't we?"

"Well normally with serial killers their first crime can be rather messy, the second and subsequent murders tend to be clinical and yet this case doesn't appear to be in any pattern. I mean the first one appears to have been planned meticulously. I mean look how he's displayed the body." He pointed to Caroline's picture, "and yet the second murder is so out of context. I think perhaps he returned to the body on the boat afterwards and just dropped the teddy bear in the water."

"I see what you mean this second murder is messy," Josephine acquiesced.

"Serial killers normally work in cycles and patterns, and it was odd there was no sexual interference in either case. It wasn't done in a lustful fashion, and yet in the first instance it appears the murderer wants to flaunt their crime," Andrew Blythe said.

"The second victim, Karen Forbes who was married with two children. A teddy bear wreath was placed by her graveside at the funeral. As far as we know the murderer sent it. I mean how sick, as if they hadn't caused the family enough grief. What do you think of that?" she asked.

"Well it suggests to me quite obviously he is very sadistic and derives great pleasure from the discomfort of others; he likes to be in control."

Josephine felt alarmed and anxious as she wondered what sort of person they were dealing with.

"Can you give me an idea of what sort of job or career this person may have?" she asked.

"I'd say we're looking for a control freak." He took a gulp of his tea and continued. "He likes something he can operate, possibly a job in computers, electronics; on those lines anyway. I'd put him at about twenty-five to forty-five years of age, white male, most possibly educated and in a white collar job."

"Anything else about his personality? I mean would he

be an exhibitionist for instance, if you say he likes to flaunt and display his victims' bodies?" Josephine asked.

"Not necessarily. He wouldn't like intrusions and might be reluctant to socialise," he replied.

"Should we be looking for a family man?"

"I can't be sure, but I don't think we are. I should imagine he'd be single and visits to the family would be regulated. What can you tell me about the victims' personalities?" he asked Josephine.

"Caroline Ryan was divorced, with a boyfriend, a reasonably good job, and her own car and flat."

"So would you say she was a strong-minded possibly aggressive, independent woman?"

"I'd say she was independent… I believe a lot of women have to be in today's world. I wouldn't necessarily say she was aggressive, maybe as strong-minded as a woman alone needs to be."

He detected a slight bitterness in her tone of voice.

"Karen Forbes," she continued "was married with children. As I said earlier, there's a possibility she was blackmailing her boss, so she'd be more than likely to be the more aggressive of the two, or perhaps she just wanted to get on in her job."

"All right, let's just say they weren't weak indecisive women. They both worked and could stand on their own feet. Would it be true to say that?" He looked at Josephine.

"Yes I'd agree with that statement," she replied. "You know Dr Blythe… "

"Call me Andrew," he interrupted.

"You spoke of 'him'. Is it possible we could be looking for a woman?"

"What makes you say that?"

"A woman was seen leaving the first victim's apartment block. We haven't been able to trace her, but it did occur to me the murderer could be a woman."

"Female serial killers are rare, although there was one in the States recently, but I'm sure we're looking for a man." He hesitated for a moment. "I'd stake my reputation on it."

Josephine stood up and walked over to the window.

"To think there's someone out there who could strike again at any time. Are they sick?"

"They could be mentally ill, antisocial or just have a lust for sadistic pleasure."

"And what about the teddy bears?" she asked looking into his pale blue eyes.

"They could be just a red herring," he replied.

Chapter 18

"**THIS NEXT SONG** is for Ann who is celebrating her twenty-first, oops, sorry, fortieth birthday today... from all your friends and we hope this birthday is 'Simply The Best!'"

Tina Turner's record began to play.

DC Sally Fletcher stood at the bar and ordered a glass of white wine. As the barman gave her the change he smiled.

"We haven't seen you here before."

"No... it's my first visit. I was supposed to meet a friend here but she hasn't turned up."

"Oh, well they're a friendly lot here anyway!" The barman quickly turned away to serve someone else.

"Yes sir... sorry to keep you waiting."

Sally walked away with her drink and put it on a nearby table. She glanced around, not quite sure of what she was supposed to be looking for, when she noticed a man smiling at her.

Oh God he thinks I'm looking at him, she thought.

He walked over to her; he was about fifty years of age and quite smartly dressed.

"You're a new face here."

"I'm waiting for a friend," Sally replied.

"Male or female?" the man asked.

"Male actually," she lied.

The man looked a bit put out.

"Oh well if he doesn't turn up, maybe I can buy you a drink later."

"Oh thanks that would be nice," Sally smiled falsely.

She didn't want to be rude, in case she needed to make

discreet enquiries about the place, but she rather liked her ploy of pretending to be waiting for another man. At least it would help ward off any unwanted attentions so that she could get on with the job in hand, whatever that was! She was tempted to get herself another drink but decided against it as she needed to stay alert. As the evening passed she got chatting to a group of women sitting at a nearby table. They invited her over saying that they hadn't seen her there before. Sally thought she'd scream if anyone else said that.

"How did you get to know about this place?" one of them asked.

"Oh well. It's rather sad actually, only do you remember Caroline Ryan who was a member here?" she asked them.

"Oh God yes a dreadful business. We all liked Caroline. Her boyfriend David was very upset. Some people said he was involved but we don't think so."

"I live near to Caroline and she told me about the club, we were going to come together but of course… " Sally Fletcher lied.

"I know; a very sad business."

"Did she come here a lot?"

"Yes, she loved the men, don't we all," one woman said nudging Sally jokingly in the ribs.

"Caroline used to go through so many of them, always got them to buy her drinks. See that man there?" She pointed to a man with fair hair standing at the bar. "She went out with him for a few weeks but dropped him when she met David. We thought he'd cause trouble, but Caroline said she'd tell his wife if he pestered her."

"What's his name?" Sally asked.

"Bob somebody or other… Bob Jenkins, that's it."

DC Fletcher went to the ladies wondering how she could attract his attention. She put a fresh coat of lipstick on and brushed her hair. She managed to stand next to him by the bar, and after she'd got her drink she purposely knocked him and the wine spilt onto the sleeve of his jacket.

"Oh, I'm so sorry," she said giving him a smile.

She took out her hanky and started to wipe away the wine.

"That's OK, let me get you another drink. White wine wasn't it?"

"Yes thanks. It's a good job it wasn't red," she remarked.

Bob Jenkins couldn't believe his luck. *She obviously fancies me* he thought to himself, *and she can't be much above thirty*.

He'd been chatting to another woman earlier, and he noticed she was coming over to him again. He wondered how he would get rid of the other woman.

He handed Sally her drink.

"Will you excuse me for a moment?" He approached the woman and said a few words to her; she turned away looking rather annoyed. He returned to Sally

"Sorry about that. Now, I think you at least owe me a dance, don't you?"

Sally agreed and they went on to the dance floor.

An hour and a few drinks later, Bob Jenkins was a little drunk, although Sally merely drank orange juice. He became rather talkative, and the conversation got around to Caroline Ryan. He said he'd dated her for a while, but omitted to mention that he was married, and that Caroline had threatened to tell his wife if he continued to pester her.

"Wasn't it awful, her murder?" Sally said sipping her

drink.

"I reckon she asked for it. She was a bit of a bitch you know, anyway let's not talk about her, let's have another dance." He started to kiss her neck.

Oh God, the things I do for the job, she thought.

"I'll have to pop to the loo," she said.

"OK darling, don't be long. I'll be waiting."

I bet you will, Sally thought.

As she was hurrying to the ladies with her head down she bumped into someone.

"Oh I'm sorry," she said.

"That's quite all right," was the reply.

It was rather dark, but even with the sound of the music Sally thought *I know that voice*.

She looked up at the man's face. It was Tom Blake, Josephine's husband.

"Oh hello," she said.

He thought she looked familiar but couldn't place her.

"Do I know you?" he asked.

"Yes sir. Detective Inspector Josephine Blake is my boss."

As she sat down next to Bob Jenkins she wondered whether she should tell her DI about her husband being at the Blue Forest Club, and yet if he told her himself and Sally kept silent it might make matters worse. She noticed he'd left the club alone and wasn't with another woman, but wondered if that was for her benefit.

As the evening was drawing to a close Bob Jenkins asked "Can I give you a lift home?"

"I've got my own car," Sally informed him.

She was anxious to get away from him, and yet was trying to recall everything he'd told her. She'd got a small note pad in her handbag on which she had jotted a few things down each time she'd gone to the loo.

He insisted on escorting her to the car park, even though there were lots of people leaving the club. As he got into his car she noted the registration number. As they were leaving the car park his car drew up alongside hers and the Blue Forest neon sign shone into his car. There on the back seat was a huge teddy bear...

Chapter 19

"SO DID YOU FANCY that man, who was chatting you up?"

"OK I suppose," she sounded vague.

"Just OK, he was bloody gorgeous!"

The woman brushed her long black hair. She mooched in her bag until she found the lipstick she wanted and started to apply it.

"I like that shade do you think it would suit me?"

"No I think it's a little dark, peach is more your shade I'd say." She opened a small shopping bag and removed a pair of tights. "These were on special offer. They're supposed to last a minimum of one month, without snagging or laddering."

"That sounds great, but I bet they were expensive."

"Not really." She wound them round each hand and started to pull them really tightly.

"Are you testing them? Although I don't suppose you'll get your money back after pulling them like that."

The woman walked towards her, as she pulled them tighter, they became taut.

"Loren what are you doing, are you drunk?"

Her voice changed from a playful tone to a croaking fear. As she put the tights around her neck she realised Loren was no longer playing the fool.

"Loren for God's sake what are you doing?" She began to sweat from fear.

She gurgled and choked as the woman pulled them even tighter, her face changed from a healthy pink to a convulsive shade of purple. Her body shook, as she tried to hit out at her assailant, but the other woman was far too strong. She began to laugh, a crazed deranged chuckle as she pulled even tighter. The victim's strength began to wane, as the last few breaths of life were squeezed out of her. She slumped to the floor with a thump.

Chapter 20

"**RICHARD MYERS** is waiting in the interview room ma'am."

"OK thanks Barnes... I'll wait till DS Hughes gets here, he shouldn't be long."

A few minutes later Bill arrived.

"Sorry to keep you waiting; are you ready to interview him?"

"In a moment, I want a quick word first, I went to see Andrew Blythe, the forensic psychologist."

"Oh yes I'd forgotten you'd seen him—any luck?" Bill asked.

"He seems to think we're definitely looking for a man, rather calculating in character, he thinks he may work in computers or electronics or something on those lines," Josephine informed him.

"How does he arrive at that conclusion?"

"Well something to do with him being a control freak and very organised and yet he said Karen Forbes' murder was out of context, being so messy."

"Well Myers has a computer in his job doesn't he... I suppose that's something to go on, and of course he's a member of the Blue Forest Club and the only one with a motive at the moment," DS Hughes added. "What does this forensic chap make of our little furry friends. Any strange sinister meaning?" he asked.

"He seems to think they could be of no consequence," Josephine answered.

"Rubbish! They must be linked in some way. He doesn't sound much good to me!"

"I disagree, I think he was very professional, I feel sure if we liaise with him, he'll be a help to us."

"Oh well, I wasn't there ma'am so I'll just have to trust your judgement."

"Yes you will, won't you Sergeant. Shall we go in?"

They entered the interview room where Richard Myers was waiting. DS Hughes started the tape.

"17th June, ten-thirty a.m., interview with Mr Richard Myers, DI Blake and DS Hughes present," he spoke into the machine and then turned to Richard Myers and continued.

"Now Mr Myers this interview is in connection with the death of Karen Forbes."

"I don't know why you've asked me to come into the station. I thought you'd got enough information when you spoke to me at work."

"Since then Mr Myers certain facts have come to light concerning this case, Karen Forbes was blackmailing you. Isn't it true that she thought a certain amount of money was being taken by yourself from your firm?" Bill remarked.

"She may have thought that but she was wrong. My record of employment has always been impeccable."

"Isn't it true that if you got her a company car she'd remain silent?"

"There was nothing to tell, she'd got no proof anyway." He raised his voice slightly.

DI Blake intervened.

"Even if she hadn't got concrete proof, if she'd have given your superiors a slight inkling or suggestion that you may be dishonest she would have put the cat amongst the pigeons. You'd have been watched closely, so any fiddle you may have had would have had to cease. You wouldn't have been able to risk it, after the seeds of suspicion had been sown. It would have benefited you to keep her happy, and put forward a suggestion that she had a company car. It wouldn't have stopped at that. She would have become greedy, wanted a rise in salary perhaps, maybe eventually even your job. She'd never have been satisfied. Don't you think that's what would have happened Mr Myers?"

He looked a little flummoxed, but tried to keep calm.

"I disagree, I'm a long-standing reliable employee. I've been there eight years. Karen Forbes had only worked there two years, they'd have known she was lying."

"She may have only been there two years, but perhaps she made an impression on them. I gather she had quite a dominant personality," Josephine remarked.

"All she cared about was number one, she walked all over people."

"You sound very bitter, you obviously didn't like the woman," Bill Hughes said.

"No I didn't, but she wasn't blackmailing me," he replied.

"You're contradicting yourself, you've just said she walked over people, what makes you think you'd be the exception?"

"Well… I… " he paused, not knowing how to reply.

"What about your private life? She knew you saw other women and threatened to tell your wife."

"That's ludicrous. Wherever did you get that information from?"

"She confided in friends. Why would she lie to them?"

"I don't know," he answered.

"How long have you been married?" DS Hughes asked.

"I've been happily married for twenty years," he stated.

"Come on admit it, it can get boring and monotonous, that's the same time my wife and I've been married, we're only human, if a pretty face comes along…" Bill suggested.

"No that's not it. Why won't you believe me?" he asked earnestly.

Josephine began "We don't believe you Mr Myers because you're a member of the Blue Forest, divorced and singles."

"How did you know that?" He looked a little flustered.

"Perhaps you shouldn't have signed your own name in the membership book," DS Hughes suggested.

"OK I've been there with a couple of friends for a drink, it's only a bit of harmless fun that's all."

"Is that why you write a false address in the book?" Josephine asked "Why not put your correct one if you've nothing to hide?"

"I just didn't want any correspondence sent to my home."

"So obviously your wife didn't know," DS Hughes commented.

"No she didn't," he admitted.

"So you're happily married. But not honest with your wife. Is that what you're saying?" Josephine asked him.

"Is your husband always honest with you or vice versa?"

"I wouldn't have thought any married couple were completely truthful to one another all the time, but my married life isn't the issue here, yours is! I don't think you're taking this seriously enough."

She reached for a large brown envelope and removed a photograph.

"I am now showing Mr Myers a photo of Karen Forbes

taken shortly after her body was found," she pushed it over to his side of the table and said, "not a pretty sight is it?"

He seemed very reluctant to look, but when he did he said shakily, "No it's horrible, but it's got nothing to do with me."

"Can you tell me your whereabouts on the night of Thursday 8th June," the Sergeant asked him.

"At what time?"

"The entire evening say from six o'clock onwards."

"Let me think… I went for a drink with a friend, I suppose I got home about eleven or thereabouts."

"Can your wife confirm the time?" DS Hughes asked.

"I think she was asleep when I arrived home, I can't remember."

"We'll have the name and address of your friends. What time did you leave them?"

"About ten-thirty I think… anyway I'm sure the bar staff can back up my story, I'm a regular." He sounded relieved.

"Karen Forbes was killed between eleven-thirty and one-thirty approximately according to the pathologist so you'd have had plenty of time to have murdered her, after you left your friends."

"But I didn't I tell you!"

"You've got a motive, even though she wasn't blackmailing you for money she wanted you to arrange a firm's car and possibly an increase in salary."

"I wasn't in a position to do that, although I may have been able to get her a car."

"I should imagine that would be worth about fifty pounds a week, when you think of what the saving would be with tax, insurance repairs and no car loan," DS Hughes remarked.

"Anyway we don't know you weren't giving her money, she told friends she was only after a car, but she probably wouldn't admit to them she wanted money," Josephine added.

"Can you tell us your whereabouts on 1st June say from seven o'clock in the evening onwards?"

"I can't remember I'd have to check my diary. I suppose I'd be at home at that time, why do you ask?"

"That's the day the first murder occurred, the victim was Caroline Ryan," she informed him.

"Oh my God I didn't know there was another murder!" He sounded genuinely shocked.

"Didn't you read it in the papers?" Bill asked.

"No… I mean I may have done… look I know I said I didn't want a lawyer present, but I've changed my mind. I'm not saying anything else till I've spoken to one."

"Interview suspended at eleven-fifteen am", DS Hughes said.

They were in the incident room some twenty minutes later, when a call came through. Josephine answered the phone.

"DI Blake… Oh hello Barnes."

"I'm phoning from Devonshire Blooms in Dartmouth, the florist here has positively identified the teddy bear wreath as hers, she made it up personally. She distinctly remembers putting freesias among the yellow tea roses."

"Well done Roger! What about the sale?"

"Cash I'm afraid, it was collected from the shop, and

there's no address."

"Just as we expected," Josephine remarked.

"She remembers the lady who ordered them, I've taken a full description. I should be back at the station within the hour."

"Can't you make it any sooner?" she asked.

"No, I wouldn't think so, I've got to wait for the next car ferry."

"Oh yes of course I'd forgotten you're at Dartmouth; don't keep us in suspense, is it a tall woman with long dark hair?"

"No sorry ma'am, the description I've got... hang on a minute." He went through his notebook until he found the page he wanted.

"Five-foot eight, possibly taller, with red curly hair about chin length, dressed in cream. Although the florist cannot remember exactly what she was wearing, she said the woman appeared to be smartly dressed."

"Right get back here as soon as you can." DI Blake put the phone down.

She relayed the conversation to DS Hughes.

"At least the height is the same as the woman leaving Caroline Ryan's."

"Maybe she wore a red wig," he suggested.

"Yes that's a possibility or the red hair could be natural and the long dark hair could have been a wig, unless of course the murderer sent someone in to order the flowers for them."

DS Hughes thought for a moment or two.

"They could have been an unsuspecting friend or possibly an accomplice."

"That could be a valid point Bill, although according to the forensic psychologist Andrew Blythe, serial killers work alone."

"He said we weren't looking for a woman. And yet two have been sighted already in connection with the case!"

When DC Barnes arrived back at the station he went straight to the DI's office.

"I'll get this statement typed ma'am and give you a copy."

When Barnes left the office Josephine sat at her desk, thinking for several minutes. She decided she really needed to talk to the woman at the florist's shop herself even though DC Barnes was good at his job and thorough in his reports.

Just at that moment DC Sally Fletcher knocked and entered the office.

"Excuse me ma'am, only I've got that report on my visit to the Blue Forest."

"Oh of course Sally. I've been tied up interviewing Richard Myers, Karen Forbes' boss. I'm going to Dartmouth shortly, but we need to discuss it. Let's go to the canteen, I could do with something to eat before I drive there."

She wiped a smear of salad cream from her mouth, as she bit into the sandwich.

"Carry on Fletcher don't mind me," she said drinking her tea.

Sally started to describe her evening at the club and how she'd got chatting to a group of women who'd known Caroline Ryan, and that they'd told her how she dated quite a few men.

"There was one man in particular that was pointed out

to me… Bob Jenkins. Apparently he'd dated her and when she ended the relationship, he became persistent. Caroline threatened to tell his wife if he didn't leave her alone."

"Sounds interesting Sally, and did he cool it?" Josephine asked.

"According to them he caused her no bother after that, and yet I thought it was the best lead we'd got as far as the club was concerned. So I took it upon myself to get to know him. I spilt a drink over his jacket to attract his attention."

"I bet that did the trick," Josephine smiled.

"Yes it worked like a dream, he got me another drink and I couldn't get rid of him all night. Still at least it gave me the opportunity to find something out."

Josephine took another gulp of tea as she looked over at the young woman sitting opposite her. She thought how very attractive DC Fletcher was with her short black hair and dark brown eyes and that she was probably the youngest woman in the club and would have had lots of men after her. She envied her youth and her dark eyelashes. Josephine had lovely eyes herself, but needed to wear mascara as her lashes were so fair. Yes, she liked the young DC with her guts and determination, she'd go far.

Sally Fletcher continued.

"Anyway he became a bit persistent about me having a lift home. I explained I'd come in my own car, but agreed to meet him there again, just to get rid of him really."

"We'll get his address from the membership book, so he should be easy to contact if we do need to speak to him."

"There's more to come actually ma'am. As the cars were leaving the car park, I drew level with his car and as he drove under the neon blue light it shone into his car, and there sitting on the back seat was a huge teddy bear," she said proudly. "I suppose it could be a coincidence, he didn't seem like a murderer to me, he just wasn't the type, mind you it's a bit frightening to think I could have gone home with him."

"Listen Sally if I'd have thought for one moment you'd be in any danger, I'd have made sure you had back-up or at least told you to take someone with you, I just wanted you to suss the place out."

"I'm sure he's not involved, it's just a feeling I've got; call it woman's intuition."

"DS Hughes can get his address from the copy we have of the members list, and he can go and speak to him. Right, I think I'll get the driver to take me to Dartmouth." She went to stand up.

"There's just one more thing I need to tell you ma'am," her face looked serious. Josephine sat back down.

"Yes… what is it?"

"I don't know whether I should mention this."

"For God's sake Sally, spit it out I'm in a hurry!"

"Well I bumped into Mr Blake there," she said meekly.

Josephine's heart came into her mouth, and her throat went dry, she wanted desperately to appear unruffled but had to ask the question.

"Was he with anyone?"

"No, just a friend I gather, a man he works with," Sally informed her.

'There's no need to keep anything from me, I'm a big girl now, you know, and we're having a trial separation."

"I'm not, I'd tell you if he was with a woman," she replied honestly.

"Did he see you?" Josephine asked.

"Yes I spoke to him. I sure there was nothing in it."

"He was at a divorced, separated and singles club, so it's obvious there must be."

Even though she felt she could trust DC Fletcher Josephine thought it unprofessional to continue this conversation about her private life.

"Anyway it doesn't matter, I've got more important things to deal with, it's of no consequence," she lied.

As she stood up she said "I'd like this kept between ourselves."

"That goes without saying ma'am."

Chapter 21

AS SHE ENTERED 'Devonshire Blooms' Josephine felt stifled. There were so many plants and flowers in such a small proximity that they used up all the air. She'd always suffered from slight hay fever and began to sneeze. A woman walked over to her.

"Can I help you?"

She took out her warrant card.

"Detective Inspector Blake, I believe my DC spoke to you earlier?"

"Yes that's right, about the teddy bear wreath."

"I don't suppose there's any doubt it came from this shop?"

"None at all. I arranged it myself and I ran out of yellow tea roses, and I distinctly remember using yellow freesias to finish it. I recognised it instantly when I was shown the photo."

"Did you speak to the person who ordered it?"

"My assistant took the order originally but I was here when it was collected."

"I know you've given a statement earlier, but can you tell me again."

"Yes the woman had red hair, that was slightly curly, it was just past the chin, I can recall it looked a little old fashioned, like a forties hairstyle."

"Could it have been a wig do you suppose?" Josephine asked.

"I couldn't say, I didn't look that closely, I can remember she wore cream, I'm not sure what she was actually wearing but she seemed to be quite expensively dressed."

"Did she mention who the flowers were for?"

"No but we normally do teddy bear wreaths for children's funerals. I can remember saying when I gave it to her, how sad it is when a child dies and she just agreed."

"If you or your assistant can remember anything else please contact us."

"Oh there was something, I could smell her perfume."

"Is that unusual?" Josephine asked.

"Yes it is, because the smell of all the flowers in the shop is so strong, it's rare to detect a fragrance on anyone, the flowers overpower the smell. Oh, and I almost forgot, she'd got a cold."

"It could have been the flowers, as you probably noticed I've been sneezing since I came into the shop," Josephine suggested.

"Her voice sounded rough and groggy as if she'd got a bad throat, I don't think it was the flowers that caused it."

Josephine handed over her card, and left the shop. She walked along the side of the River Dart, recalling when she and Tom would take a boat out for the day. They'd take a picnic basket and would pull over to the bank if they saw a spot they fancied; those were idyllic days and she wondered if things would ever be the same again. Her mind went back to her conversation with DC Fletcher as she considered the possibility he may have someone else. His visit to the club could just have been a one-off but why did he go there if not to meet someone. Had a friend persuaded him to go? She kept turning different possibilities over and over in her mind till she thought she'd go mad. Deciding what was needed was a cup of tea, she made her way to the Riverside Cafe and watched the boats for a while, before she returned to the station.

The following day Josephine was discussing with DS Hughes and the rest of the team the sighting of yet another woman. They went over the possibilities again that it could have been the same woman seen leaving Kew Gardens and disguising herself in a wig.

"Of course," Josephine started to speak, "we don't know for certain that the dark-haired woman seen leaving the flats was connected with the murder at all. The only thing that is pretty definite is that the other residents didn't know her. But we do know the second woman must be involved as the teddy bear wreath she collected was placed at Karen Forbes grave."

"Do you think ma'am it's possible the murderer got the woman to go in and buy it for him, and she was an unsuspecting accomplice." DC Barnes suggested.

"Yes that's feasible Barnes, he could have told her to pay cash and not give an address."

"Wouldn't she have been suspicious that he didn't want it delivered?" Bill asked.

"I suppose he could have said it was for a child that was close to him, and he preferred to take it to the funeral personally. That is if it is a male we're looking for."

"Surely a close friend or relative wouldn't have gone into the shop on his behalf because they'd want to know the details of the funeral."

"There's always the possibility the red-haired woman who collected the flowers was the murderer," Josephine said.

"Now what happened when you spoke to Bob Jenkins?" she asked Bill.

"He did date Caroline Ryan, obviously his wife didn't

know, lucky for him she wasn't in when I called at his house. He said he was disappointed when she finished with him, but was quite adamant he didn't pester her to go back out with him."

"Well he wouldn't admit to that anyway," DC Fletcher commented.

"He seems to have an alibi for both nights in question, Karen Forbes' death and Caroline Ryan's. I've got to check them though. I've run him through the computer and he's got no form."

"What about the teddy bear I saw in the back of his car?" Sally asked.

"When I mentioned it to him he seemed shocked and surprised that I knew about it. Apparently it was a birthday present for his young daughter. He'd bought it after work and gone straight to the Blue Forest Club without going home."

"He'd have to say it was a present to cover himself," DC Fletcher remarked.

"Although he took me into the bedroom, to verify his story, and it was on his daughter's bed it looked new, and he also had the receipt. It was a white and quite large, does that sound like the one you spotted in the back of his car?"

"Well it was big and light in colour. I couldn't say if it was white but I still don't trust the man," she replied.

"Just because he chatted you up Detective Constable?" DS Hughes said in a very chauvinistic manner.

Josephine intervened.

"All right, he's a ladies' man, and he plays around. That doesn't make him a murderer. Mind you he knew Caroline Ryan, he is a member of the Blue Forest and he's bought a teddy bear so obviously there's always the possibility he's involved. Get his alibis checked thoroughly before we dismiss him Bill."

When she arrived home that evening Josephine smelt cigar smoke the moment she'd opened the front door. As she walked into the lounge there was Tom with his feet up in his favourite chair gazing out to sea. He looked very contented as he puffed on his cigar.

"How did you get in? I didn't think you'd got a key." Josephine asked.

"I found the spare one in the hiding place. I don't know, you a Detective Inspector. Not very hot on security are you? Whatever would the neighbourhood watch think," he laughed.

"Well you can put it back where you found it when you leave."

"Tomorrow morning all right?"

"No, right now!"

He knew by the look on Josephine's face, that the young DC had told her she'd seen him at the club.

"OK I admit I was there," he started "I was going to tell you about it."

"Well you're bound to say that, now that she's seen you."

"Look a mate of mine was a member, and he offered to sign me in. I wasn't on the look out for anyone," he tried to sound reassuring.

"Well even if you were on the pull it's no business of mine," she lied as she walked into the kitchen.

He got up from his chair and followed her.

"Of course it's your business, we're not divorced, we're not even legally separated… look Jo… " He put his hands on her shoulders and turned her round to face him. "This is ridiculous, I've got no-one else and I'm not looking for anyone either… if you can't trust me after all these years…"

She thought for a moment about her visit to Andrew Blythe, and how attractive she'd found him.

"But you must be attracted to other women, Tom you're only human."

"Well yes… if you put it like that but not to the extent of going to bed with anyone. Or even asking them out for that matter."

"You've taken your secretary out."

"What a stupid thing to say. She's fifty-eight, adores her husband and if you'd really like to know she's always nagging me to sort things out with you."

She realised what a childish thing that was to say to him. Josephine wanted to believe him, she did believe him, then what was holding her back.

"Leave the dinner." he said as he started to kiss her neck.

"I don't think we ought to Tom."

"Why ever not, Jessica won't be coming back I've bribed her with ten pounds, so she's gone to the cinema with a friend." He untied her blouse and started to kiss her breasts.

"God it's been ages," he sighed.

"Is this just to satisfy your sexual urge?" she asked.

"Of course it's not, we've always had a good sex life, I've missed it."

"Oh just it, not me!"

"All right, I've missed you and the sex, why separate them."

She was tempted to pull away, but she succumbed. They went into the bedroom and made love on top of the bed. It wasn't any more passionate than usual, but having familiar sex with a man whose body she'd known for the last twenty years. He knew exactly what she enjoyed and all the right things to do to arouse her.

They'd made love and it was good and she felt satisfied and content. Yet while they were making love she'd fantasised about Andrew Blythe. This didn't necessarily disturb her, as she'd occasionally fantasised over the years. Josephine felt close to Tom as she lay in his arms afterwards, there was no doubt she still loved him, and yet there was a small nagging doubt in the back of her mind.

She hadn't eaten for hours and felt ravenous so she went downstairs and prepared some sandwiches and got a bottle of wine from the fridge and took them back to bed on a tray.

"How romantic, feeding me in the bedroom," Tom said playfully.

It was a pleasant evening; they stayed in bed eating and drinking and talking about the case. Josephine didn't normally discuss her work with Tom but she felt the need to unburden herself.

At around eleven-thirty Tom said "I might as well stay the night, there's no point in me going to Mum's, I'll phone her."

"I suppose you shouldn't drive after drinking that wine," she said.

"Do you think I should move back in permanently?" Tom said hesitantly.

"We've had a lovely evening, because we haven't seen one another for over a week and we haven't made love for ages. But if you come back Tom the relationship will go stale and mundane again and we'll start taking each other for granted."

"Don't all married couples?" Tom replied.

"I suppose they do, tonight's been great but it won't be like this all the time."

He jumped out of bed and started to get dressed.

"Honestly Jo… there are times when I think you're living in 'cloud cuckoo land'. You're an intelligent woman, if anyone's seen the sordid side of life you have in your job. Things do get humdrum, we're not youngsters any more for God's sake!" He finished dressing and grabbed his car keys.

"Do you think you should drive after all that wine?" she asked.

"That's my problem, sort yourself out Jo. I won't be around for ever!" He slammed the front door.

She was tempted to go after him but just stood and watched him drive away. She knew in her own mind that things would have to be sorted out. Tom was a good man, and she was being unreasonable. *What the hell's wrong with me?* she thought. She reached for the remote control and turned the television on. Just at that moment the phone rang; she glanced at the clock. It was nearly midnight! As she picked up the phone she said automatically,

"Is that you Jessica?"

"No ma'am its Bill. Sorry to ring you so late only there's been another murder!"

Chapter 22

THE HOUSE WAS SITUATED near to Anstey's Cove, which was one of Josephine's favourite haunts, so she found it odd that she should now be visiting the area in such solemn circumstances. It was quite an elegant town house with Regency style windows. When DI Blake arrived there were several police cars outside with their blue lights flashing and the front garden was being cordoned off with tape. There were lots of neighbours and people about, despite the time. They appeared to be enjoying the spectacle. Josephine was the last to arrive at the scene of the crime. DS Hughes and the team had been there for twenty minutes and also John Gardner the forensic pathologist; she was met at the doorway by the sergeant.

"The Chief won't like this—another one, and no signs of an arrest yet."

"I'm not exactly overjoyed by the situation either, Bill. What more can we do? I phoned the forensic psychologist Andrew Blythe before I left. He's on his way.

"Do we need him?" DS Hughes asked.

"I think we do, he said he could tell more about the murderer if he was at the scene of the crime, he's only had the pictures and reports of the other two murders to go on," Josephine replied. "Have we got a name?"

"Yes it's a Sylvia Gordon. I've spoken to her next door neighbour a Mrs Fay Romsley, she's a good friend apparently, although I've not taken a proper statement yet. She informs me that Sylvia Gordon was divorced with one married son who lives in Plymouth, they're trying to contact him now."

148

"It seems an expensive house to run for a woman alone," Josephine remarked.

"Well according to Mrs Romsley, Sylvia's husband was quite affluent and had a high powered job and when they divorced he left her the house, she didn't have a mortgage but she does work so probably just had to pay the upkeep and bills."

As Josephine walked down the hallway she noticed that the house contained one or two nice pieces. There was a French Ormolu clock on the hall table, and an exquisite oil painting, and it was decorated very expensively.

"The body's upstairs," the Sergeant informed her.

Sylvia Gordon's body was sitting upright on the bed with her head against the headboard. At a first glance it appeared she had been strangled. Her eyes were open and staring, they looked blank and glassy; a blue ribbon was tied neatly around her neck in a bow, and yet beneath it there was a considerable amount of bruising as the ribbon wasn't wide enough to cover up the marks. She had long scratch marks on her right cheek; they were quite deep and had bled, they ran from her eye right down to her chin. It looked as if a cat had attacked her. She wore a pale blue nightie, and as expected a teddy bear sat next to her on the bed.

It was a much larger bear than those left at the other two murders and it appeared to be older. It had glass eyes that were staring and blank like the victim's. Josephine Blake shivered; it was uncanny how the two expressions were so similar. She wondered what Andrew Blythe would deduce from it all.

On the bed lay a piece of paper, Josephine was given

plastic gloves to wear and she picked it up and read it out loud "IF YOU GO DOWN IN THE WOODS TODAY YOU'RE SURE OF A BIG SURPRISE."

"That's the first line of the 'Teddy Bears Picnic', if I'm not mistaken."

John Gardner the Pathologist came over to her.

"I've examined the body. Not in detail you understand, but as far as I can tell she's been dead about four hours."

"So that would make time of death say approximately between seven p.m. and nine p.m. this evening," Josephine said.

He nodded in agreement.

"Obviously death by strangulation is my first impression but I can give you a more thorough report when I get back to the lab."

"How did she come to be found?" DI Blake asked a PC standing nearby.

"Her neighbour had a key ma'am, she'd tried to phone her earlier this evening but got no reply, and since the light was on, she became a little concerned, that perhaps Mrs Gordon was ill. According to Mrs Romsley she only used the key to let the gas man in, or say as a spare if Mrs Gordon had lost hers," he informed her.

Just at that moment Dr Andrew Blythe came into the room; he walked straight over to the bed where the body lay, without even acknowledging Josephine or any of her team. He looked long and hard at the victim for several minutes and appeared to be in some sort of a trance.

When his concentration seemed to lapse Josephine said "I'm sorry I had to call you out at this time of night, only you did say you wanted to be at the scene if another murder occurred."

He turned and smiled.

"That's not a problem. I apologise if I seemed oblivious to you when I came in—I felt that I needed to pick up any sort of vibes. I need to concentrate on the scene, as the murderer would have left it, to try and imagine what he may have been feeling."

"Oh yes I can appreciate that," Josephine lied. "Can you tell us anything now, or do you need more time?"

"As you can see her body's been displayed, her legs have been slightly opened and her arms, she's in the same position as the bear. Even the blue ribbon around her neck matches the nightdress and her facial expression is uncannily similar to that of the bear."

"That was the first thing I noticed," Josephine told him.

"I'd say he took several pieces of ribbon with him, and used the one needed to match the victim's attire. I also believe he had several teddy bears, and also left the one that looked most like his victim. This bear appears to be rather old, it could be an antique and quite valuable, although I suppose you need to get that confirmed by an expert. I'm of the opinion the murderer has a real love of teddy bears and could be a collector, that being the case I should imagine he'd be loathe to part with this one."

"What do you make of the scratch marks on her face?" Josephine asked.

"Perhaps she fought for her life more than past victims, and he regarded her life as more precious."

"But surely all human life is precious," Josephine remarked.

"Yes, but not to him, obviously she wouldn't have been

spared, but he maybe admired her courage and the fight she put up, so he decided her life was worth a better teddy bear. I know it sounds odd, but I feel he hates parting with his bears, but that they have to give their life in exchange for a bear."

Josephine wondered what must have gone through this woman's mind as she fought for her life, she felt sick inside.

"You keep saying 'he.' Are you still convinced it's a man?" she asked.

"Yes I am. He may have killed her somewhere else in the room, I know we won't know that for certain until we get the Pathologist's report, but it would take a certain amount of strength to put her onto the bed. She wasn't a small woman."

"Well women are stronger nowadays," Josephine suggested.

"I suppose it's a possibility." He didn't sound convinced.

"A red-haired woman ordered the flowers that were sent to Karen Forbes' funeral and look at these scratch marks, it seems to me they were made with long nails, being so deep; women's are nearly always longer and sharper than men's."

Dr Blythe studied the paper on the bed.

"This note is very interesting. It doesn't just tie in with the bears, I believe the murderer is trying to tell us something. 'THE SURPRISE'—maybe another body. When he says 'TONIGHT'—it's after midnight now, but he wouldn't have thought that this body would have been discovered so soon. He can't have known that the neighbour had a key to the house, and he most probably thought she'd lay undiscovered until the next day or even later. I'd say he's planning another murder. Let's think where the woods are located in the area."

"There's a wood leading down to Anstey's Cove, but I feel that's too close to here. They'd obviously know there would be a considerable police presence where she was found. Also there's a wooded area where I live at Babbacombe leading down to the beach, and also around Meadfoot."

Josephine stopped talking and seemed deep in thought. "When I was a child I used to love the woods at Cockington, they were so magical. I really believed the fairies lived there and they've never changed, they're as unspoilt now as they've always been. I could just imagine teddy bears having a picnic there… It's just a hunch and yet… "

"Don't knock it; you'd be surprised, a woman's intuition can prove more reliable than proven logic at times," he assured her.

"I'll set Bill on to it straight away and have all the other wooded areas searched thoroughly."

Josephine didn't get to bed until two-thirty that morning, and she woke at seven o'clock in the morning feeling exhausted and sweaty. The few hours sleep she did manage were disturbing and unsettling; all she dreamt about were teddy bears sitting around a table in the woods drinking, eating and laughing in a demented and crazed way, and women screaming and frantically fighting for life. She felt physically ill, and needed to stay in bed. It took all the will power she could muster to dress and shower, and after several cups of coffee she felt slightly regenerated.

When she finally arrived at the station, she organised a search of all the woods in the area and also arranged for

Sylvia Gordon's neighbours to be interviewed to see if they could remember anyone leaving her house.

DC Barnes was given the task of researching the history of the teddy bear and contacting societies and clubs. The information he acquired was that 'teddy bears' were used to decorate the tables at Theodore Roosevelt's daughters' wedding. Apparently he had refused to kill a bear cub in 1902, and the newspapers had nicknamed it Teddy's bear. Antique bears could fetch up to two thousand pounds in auction, and a much sought after make was manufactured by a Germany company called Steiff. The original bear was designed in 1903; although there were many copies of the Steiff bear on the market, the limbs of the authentic ones were swivel jointed, but in the case of copies the limbs were simply stitched to the body. After examination by an expert it was found the bear left by Sylvia Gordon's body was quite old, and valued at about five hundred pounds.

DI Blake passed this information on to Andrew Blythe. He found the fact that genuine teddy bears had movable joints, much like the human body, of significance.

The following day John Gardner asked to see Josephine at the laboratory.

"We've examined her face in detail, they were definitely nails that made the marks, and from the size of the scratches they were long and pointed."

"I knew they were women's nails all along, as men's are shorter, even though the forensic psychologist was adamant it was a man," Josephine remarked.

"I'm afraid I've got some results that may prove different,"

John Gardner added.

She waited in anticipation.

"We found traces of semen on her legs and in her vagina. I'd say she'd had sexual intercourse possibly an hour or so before death occurred."

"This is the first one we've come across, was she raped?" Josephine inquired.

"I doubt that very much, her vagina was moist when she was penetrated, which leads me to believe she was aroused. There is no damage to the walls of the vagina or uterus, supporting the fact that no undue force was used."

"So she obviously knew the murderer quite well, and could have been having a relationship with him. Her name is not entered in the Blue Forest membership book, it doesn't appear that she frequented the place. Oh God I'm so confused! Scratch marks possibly inflicted by a woman, and yet she had sex with a man!"

"There's one other thing, she had an appointment card in her handbag to visit a clinic for sexual related diseases, so we tested her, and she was HIV positive."

"How uncanny, so if it was her murderer that had sex with her, she may have unknowingly have got revenge on him, by giving him a sort of death sentence in return."

When she arrived back at the station the Chief barged into her office and threw two newspapers on her desk.

"Have you seen this?" he said in an exasperated manner.

"No sir, I've been at the path lab all morning," she was a little flummoxed as she picked up the local newspaper first. The first page headline said 'SERIAL KILLER STRIKES

AGAIN IN TORQUAY". It read:-

"IF THE CID IN TORBAY DON'T FIND THIS MANIAC SOON, IT COULD BE DEVASTATING FOR THE TORBAY TOURIST BOARD, AS HOLIDAY MAKERS STEER CLEAR OF THIS ONCE POPULAR SEASIDE RESORT"

"Even the nationals have got hold of it." He pointed to an article in the other newspaper; although it wasn't on the front page it was a fairly big piece. She read out an extract "CAN WE NO LONGER ESCAPE FROM HIGH CRIME CITIES TO THE TRANQUILLITY OF THE SEA SIDE, AS THE TORBAY POLICE DEPARTMENT USE ALL THEIR RESOURCES IN THE FIGHT TO STOP CRIME."

"That's unfair. This isn't a high crime area, it's only this serial killer," she commented.

"Whenever have you known the media to be fair, Detective Inspector? I'm giving you extra manpower and you've got one more week. If you don't make an arrest in that time you're off the case!"

He didn't wait for her reply as he slammed the door and left.

She assembled the team in the incident room.

"Right I suppose you've all heard the Chief is on the warpath, and the press are doing us no favours at the moment. I've got one week left and then I'm being taken off the case."

They all remained silent.

"I've been to see the forensic pathologist; Sylvia Gordon had sexual intercourse about an hour before she was killed, so it's quite feasible she knew her murderer, and yet the scratch marks on her face indicate it could be a woman."

DC Barnes was the first of the team to speak.

"I've got a report here from a PC who questioned the neighbours, one who lives opposite said he saw a woman with short blonde hair leaving Sylvia Gordon's house at about nine o'clock."

"That could be at least half an hour to an hour after her death, she could be our murderer."

"But what about the semen found on the body?" DS Hughes asked.

"Then there's only one possibility—it must have been a man dressed as a woman!" Josephine remarked.

"Is the neighbour's statement reliable?" the Sergeant asked Barnes.

"Well, the PC said he was a young man, with good eyesight and he was certain it was a woman."

"I wonder if this is the first time he's had sex with Sylvia Gordon. Perhaps he left the expensive teddy bear as a thank you for the pleasure she'd given him and not just her life?" Josephine said thoughtfully.

Just at that moment the duty sergeant came in from the front desk.

"Excuse me ma'am, only I've got a Mr Myers at reception, he seems very agitated, and says he'll only speak to yourself or DS Hughes."

"Thanks Sergeant. Put him in an interview room if one is free, and we'll be there shortly," Josephine answered.

"Now I wonder what he wants?" DS Hughes rubbed his chin.

"Well there's only one way to find out." Josephine left the incident room followed by Bill.

Richard Myers looked in a terrible state; his face was pale and sweaty and his eyes looked sunken and dark. He asked if he could smoke and lit a cigarette with his shaking hand.

Josephine decided not to use the hard approach. "Would you like a cup of tea Mr Myers?"

"Oh yes… I would… thanks."

A PC bought three paper cups of tea into the room.

"Did you know there's been another murder?" DS Hughes asked.

"Yes I read it in the paper." His voice sounded groggy.

"So why have you come to see us Mr Myers?" DS Hughes asked.

"Look, I want to tell you the truth."

"About the murders?" DI Blake asked.

"No… not about those. I mean about Sylvia."

"I think we'd better put a tape in to record the interview. Do you want a lawyer present Mr Myers?" the Sergeant asked.

"I've not done anything wrong, I mean do I need one?"

"It all depends on what you've got to tell us," Josephine answered.

"I was having an affair with Sylvia Gordon," he admitted.

"You told us that what Karen Forbes knew about you was rubbish, and that you were faithful to your wife," Josephine stated.

"OK I lied, I'll come clean, Karen Forbes did know I'd got another woman, and also that I was getting extra money from the firm."

"So she was blackmailing you?" DS Hughes suggested.

"Well, no I wouldn't exactly call it blackmail, all I had to arrange was for her to get a company car. I'd have been able to swing that for her and she also wanted a rise in salary. She wasn't demanding money off me personally," he informed them.

"No, but she may have got round to that eventually, once she'd got the car and the rise. She wouldn't have been content for long. Perhaps that's why you had to get rid of her," Josephine suggested.

"No, I tell you, you're wrong. I didn't like Karen Forbes, I was amazed how she'd got all the information about me. She must have been watching me like a hawk, she seemed to know all my movements; in fact I hated the woman, but I didn't murder her!"

"Did you see Sylvia Gordon last night?"

"Yes, I told my wife I was working late and I went to her house at six-thirty; we had a drink and something to eat and then we made love."

"What time did you leave?"

"About eight o'clock I think."

"Not much time is it for a drink a meal and sex, only one and a half hours," DS Hughes suggested.

"She just made me a sandwich, I had to get back, because I'd told my wife I wouldn't be too late."

"I suppose Sylvia didn't like you running back to the 'little woman'," DS Hughes remarked, "was she angry with you and that's why you murdered her?"

"Oh my God! You think I killed her as well," he shouted. "Most times I'd stay longer and I took her out when I could, it was just on that particular night I had to get home."

"Did you meet her at the Blue Forest?" Josephine asked.

"No it was some pub in Paignton that runs a divorced and singles night once a week, I've known her about six months."

"What do you think of teddy bears?" DS Hughes asked.

"I don't know what you mean… Oh hang on, I read it in the papers, he's leaving one at the murders," he replied.

"Why do you say 'he'?"

"Well I don't know, I just assumed it was a man."

"You knew the second victim, Karen Forbes. Sylvia Gordon, victim number three, had sex with you shortly before she died, and you want us to believe you're not involved?" Josephine stated.

"I didn't know the first victim," he replied nervously.

"She was a member of the Blue Forest club so you may have known her."

"Look, I'm a happily married man," he said as he took out his wallet and showed them a picture which was presumably his wife and daughter.

"So happy in fact that you're having sex and dating another woman on a regular basis," Josephine said as she picked up the photo.

The older woman in the picture, Mrs Myers, had short blonde hair.

"Tell me, was your wife in when you arrived home?"

"No, she'd gone to her mother's; she'd left a note saying she'd be home at about nine-thirty," he informed them.

"So she can't confirm the time you arrived?" Josephine continued.

"No… I don't suppose she can … Look I think I'd better have a solicitor. I know it looks bad but I didn't kill her. I was really fond of Sylvia."

"How can you say that when you're a happily married man?" Josephine replied.

"We shall be obtaining a warrant to search your home."

"You can't do that, my wife will wonder what's going on."

"It will have to come out eventually, in the meantime if you want to, telephone her or your solicitor, as we'll be keeping you in custody for twenty-four hours."

"By the way Mr Myers did you always use protection when you had sex with Sylvia Gordon?" DS Hughes asked.

"Well... sometimes... I... "

"You didn't the last time you visited her, did you?"

"I can't remember," he replied.

"Semen was found in her vagina and on her body. We'll have to carry out a DNA test to determine if it was your semen; you will also have an HIV test."

"There's no need for that," Richard Myers said adamantly.

"Oh I think there is; you see, Sylvia Gordon was HIV positive," Josephine informed him. "End of interview, time two-fifteen p.m." She turned off the tape recorder.

Josephine was having a late lunch in the canteen with DS Hughes. There wasn't a lot left, although she was that hungry she'd settle for anything.

"The woman seen leaving Sylvia Gordon's house had short blonde hair and so does Richard Myers' wife, could there be a link do you think?" Bill said as he tucked into some dubious-looking chips.

"Lots of women have short blonde hair, it's probably just a coincidence, still I suppose we could talk to her. Let's assume he's telling the truth, and he had sex and left her alive and well and the murderer came in afterwards. There were no signs of a break-in, so she must have known the person and let them in," Josephine suggested.

"She could have thought it was Myers returning, perhaps she thought he'd left something," Bill added.

"I think we'll interview the wife," Josephine said.

Chapter 23

THEY PULLED UP outside Richard Myers' house; it had just had a new drive laid.

"This looks smart," Bill said.

"Yes costly too, he's probably embezzling more money than we realise," Josephine commented.

Mrs Myers seemed genuinely alarmed and frightened that her husband was being held in custody.

"You've got the wrong person. We've always been happily married, and I've satisfied him sexually."

"He tells us you weren't here when he arrived home?" DS Hughes said.

"That's right; when I got back from my mother's house he was here," she replied.

"How did your husband seem?"

"Quite well, but tired. We had some supper and went to bed about eleven-thirty. He didn't act like a man who's just murdered someone if that's what you mean," she said defensively.

"We'll be getting a warrant to search the house, but could you tell us Mrs Myers, do you have any teddy bears in the house?" DS Hughes inquired.

"What an odd question, I've still got my daughter's bear that she had as a child. She's at university now but I couldn't part with it." She took them to her daughter's room and showed them the bear

"Get your warrant, but you won't find anything here."

As they were leaving Josephine turned to Bill and said

"Did you notice her nails? They were short, not the long pointed ones that clawed at Sylvia Gordon's face."

"I suppose she could have cut them." Bill suggested.

"I don't think so Bill, women do take pride in their hands. It takes an age to grow nails to a decent length. I know women who think a broken nail is a catastrophe."

"But surely you'd cut them if you knew you were a suspect in a murder case," Bill remarked.

"Her nails were so short I think she bites them."

"Mind you, the jealous wife. Maybe she knew he was having an affair and followed him there. Perhaps she was anxious and angry waiting, knowing he was inside making love to another woman and went into the house after he'd left. Of course there are the other two victims to consider. We'll have to get a statement as to where she was on those dates," Bill said.

"I think we'll get Bob Jenkins checked out as well, you know the one DC Fletcher met at the Blue Forest," Josephine added. As they were driving back, her mobile phone began to ring. She pulled up the aerial.

"DI Blake… yes Barnes, we're not far from there now… we'll be right over." She put the phone down and turned to Bill. "My hunch proved right; they've found a body in the woods at Cockington."

"This is getting out of control. No woman in Torquay will feel safe to go out at night." Bill sighed.

"This isn't a woman's body Bill. It's a man. I suppose that's what the murderer meant by a 'Big Surprise'."

When they arrived at the scene Josephine felt sad. She'd loved those woods as a child, and now she was about to see a murdered corpse there. John Gardner came over to her.

"When did you receive the note?" he asked.

"It was discovered on the bed of the last victim just over two days ago. Why?"

"Because this man has been dead for at least three weeks. The body has started to decompose and is riddled with insects. It's not a pretty sight."

She walked over with him to the body. It was just as he'd described. It looked like something out of a horror film.

"There's a bad injury at the back of his head which could have killed him instantly but he was strangled afterwards, I suppose just to make sure he was dead. Forensic are checking the area now. They've found a partly opened packet of condoms nearby. They may have belonged to him which could suggest he was about to have sex, but until his fingerprints have been checked against those on the packet we won't know for certain."

DS Hughes was with the forensic team as they were sifting through the undergrowth and leaves. After several minutes he came over to DI Blake.

"You'll never believe what we've just found."

He was just about to tell her when she interrupted him.

"Let me guess… teddy bears sitting around a table."

"How did you know?" he asked.

"It was obvious. The note he left about the Teddy Bears Picnic by Jimmy Kennedy. 'IF YOU GO DOWN TO THE WOODS TODAY YOU'RE SURE OF A BIG SURPRISE. IF YOU GO DOWN IN THE WOODS TODAY YOU'LL HARDLY BELIEVE YOUR EYES'. He knew we'd be shocked to find a man's body. I don't know whether Andrew Blythe would agree with me but I was convinced that's how he'd display the bears."

As she walked over the scene was just how she'd imagined it. A small table only about a foot high, possibly a child's, with three teddy bears sitting around with toy cups and saucers on the table. forensic dusted them down.

"No prints ma'am but they haven't been here as long as the body, they're in good condition. I know the surrounding trees would possibly protect them from the rain, but they'd still have been soiled and had insects on them. I'd say they'd only been here a day or so." DC Fletcher came over to Josephine.

"We can't seem to contact Dr Blythe ma'am."

"We'll have to make sure forensic take plenty of pictures of the body and the table with the bears, and he'll have to make the best deduction he can from them."

Andrew Blythe arrived at the station the following day. Josephine took him to the incident room and showed him the photos of the male victim found in the wood, with the teddy bears around the table left nearby.

"May I tell you what I deduced from this, only from an amateur's point of view of course."

"By all means, go ahead," he replied, his blue eyes smiling at her.

"First let me tell you we discovered that the reason the body wasn't discovered earlier, was that the victim Brian Jarvis, in his early thirties, was here looking for casual work. He'd just booked in bed and breakfast so they wouldn't be surprised that he never returned. He didn't have close family, he wasn't married, but he did have a father in the Midlands; he'd probably assumed he'd found work when he didn't return. So obviously he wasn't reported missing, so there was nothing about the murder mentioned in the paper. I feel that this killer wants all their crimes and actions reported, and was possibly concerned that this hadn't been. That's why the note was left to let us know there was another body. Because it was in the woods and had lain there a few weeks the body had started to decompose slightly and yet the bears were an afterthought to tie in with the 'Teddy Bears Picnic'. forensic confirmed that they'd only been there a day or so." Andrew Blythe walked over to the window.

"I agree with everything you've said, in fact Detective Inspector Blake, I think you should take up psychology. One thing that does puzzle me is that this victim is a man, as a rule serial killers' victims are the same sex."

"One thing's for certain, I've got just under a week left then I'm off the case. I feel so desperate I need all the help I can get," she said glumly.

"Give me a profile on the suspects you have, or anyone who you think may be even remotely involved, I'll examine them thoroughly and see if they tie up with my evaluation of the murderer."

She gave him all the information she had on David Vane, Karen Forbes' friends, Bob Jenkins, Richard Myers who was pretty high on their list and also Mrs Myers. After he'd left DS Hughes came in.

"Any luck?" he asked.

"I've given Andrew Blythe details of all the people that are involved in the hope he may unearth something, but I'm not that confident. He was as surprised and confused as we are about the latest victim being a man."

"But when you think of it he isn't the latest is he? If forensic's tests are fairly accurate and the body's been there say three to four weeks, Caroline Ryan was murdered three weeks ago, so he could be our first victim, or possibly the second," DS Hughes commented.

"You've worked that out well, Bill, that's a good point. So we have a first victim that is male, but no teddy bear left there originally. The display of teddies and the table was probably put there after Sylvia Gordon's murder. So this one seems completely out of context, but it was obviously done by the same person. I tell you what Bill, if you could get the two pubs in Cockington checked to see if this Brian Jarvis had gone in there for a drink. I suppose he looks pretty unrecognisable now," Josephine said.

"He had a passport on him; I'll get copies of the photo distributed to see if anyone recognises him," DS Hughes informed her.

"Get that checked out then Bill, we need as much manpower as we can get. I've only got a few days left. I also think we ought to get Sylvia Gordon's background checked thoroughly. The fact she had AIDS could indicate she slept around, or had just been unlucky and contracted it from someone she was having a regular relationship with. Get her medical background looked into; there's always the possibility she could have been infected from a blood transfusion."

"I'll get on to that straight away, and let you know the moment we've got something." He left the room.

God he seems keen Josephine thought. *Maybe he's just as worried as I am of being taken off the case.*

After questioning a large number of residents who lived around Anstey's Cove, they received some information which could possibly be their first real breakthrough. Someone had spotted a red Fiesta parked outside Sylvia

Gordon's house, and noticed someone leave the house at around the time she was murdered, and drive away. The man in question was walking his dog at the time, and did manage to recall the first part of the registration, G315. He was certain of the make and model of the car as his wife also owned a Fiesta. DS Hughes had a search done on all the cars of that year and there were four listed in the Torbay area. One belonged to a young man whose father had bought it as a twenty-first present for him, the other car was registered to a Mr Gordon Smythe who was seventy years of age, and only used it on rare occasions. The third person to be questioned who drove a similar vehicle was a Mr Robert Styles. They thought that perhaps this one was more promising, but unfortunately he had a watertight alibi for the evening of Sylvia Gordon's death. It was gone into with a fine toothed comb, and it checked out. It would have been virtually impossible that the car seen leaving Mrs Gordon's house belonged to him. The last person they questioned was a Mrs Susan James who lived in Chelston; her red Fiesta's registration was G315 RFT. When she was asked about her whereabouts on the night in question she was loath to say where she was, but nevertheless was adamant she didn't take her car. DI Blake decided to have her brought into the station.

Susan James walked into the interview room; she was a tall attractive looking woman about mid-forties with long black hair, and dark eyes with curved-shaped brows. Her face looked really familiar to Josephine but she couldn't think why.

"I really don't know why you've asked me to come here," she said, a little dismayed. Josephine didn't answer her and just said

"If you'd like to sit down. We need to ask you some questions. I'm DI Blake and this is DS Hughes; would you like a solicitor present?"

"No I don't need one. I've nothing to hide."

"Your car was seen leaving a murder victim's house last Thursday, a Mrs Sylvia Gordon."

"How do you know it was my car? There's a lot of Fiestas about," she asked.

"The witness who spotted the car could only remember the first part of the number and it was put through the computer, and yours and another three came up on the computer in this area," Josephine informed her.

"Well, what about the others, have they been questioned?"

"They have, and if you can tell us where you were that evening and your alibi is confirmed, then you will be eliminated from our enquiries," DS Hughes added.

"What I was doing that evening is my business; I can assure you I'd nothing whatsoever to do with the murder."

"This last victim is one of many, I suppose you've read about it in the papers," DS Hughes said.

"Oh yes 'The Teddy Bear Murders', that was the headline. The press says it's a sadistic serial killer. You ought to be out there looking for him. Not pestering innocent people," Susan James said resolutely.

"The fact that you're refusing to reveal where you were that evening is making matters worse for you. I suggest you go and think about the situation you're in very carefully," Josephine advised her.

"Well surely you're looking for a man, he's just murdering women."

"There has been a male victim and apart from which a

woman has been sighted in the vicinity of the murders," DS Hughes informed her.

"Have you bought any flowers lately?" Josephine asked. The woman didn't flinch at all. Either she was completely ignorant as to what DI Blake was talking about or was a master of keeping her cool.

"I don't know what you mean."

"A woman sent a teddy bear wreath of yellow roses to one of the victims' funerals. Can you imagine how her husband and children felt?"

The woman's expression was serious; she looked suddenly very sad.

"How awful. How could anyone do such a thing?" She suddenly realised that the Detective had meant her.

"Look I don't know who this sick pervert is, but it's not me—I'm not saying another word till I've had legal advice."

Some thirty minutes or so later Josephine was in the incident room with Bill.

"She seemed genuinely shocked when you mentioned the wreath, she must be an excellent actress if she did know about it," Bill stated.

"She did appear to be sincere, although she may have prepared herself beforehand. Remember if she is the murderer, she'd need to be calm and collected to carry all those things out,"

"What about the hair?" Bill asked.

"Well if it was Susan James that was seen leaving Caroline Ryan's apartment it could have been her own hair, and maybe she wore a red wig when she ordered the flowers from the florist."

"Yes but the woman seen leaving Sylvia Gordon's house

had short blonde hair," DS Hughes interrupted her flow.

"Although she has long hair you'd be surprised, if it was gelled or wet and gripped close to her head, she could easily have put a wig on top of it. You'd be amazed at what women can do to their hair nowadays," she informed him.

"Obviously she's got something to hide if she won't tell us where she was that night."

Josephine contemplated for a few moments.

"I'd have thought she'd have concocted some sort of a story or alibi if she was that clever. The fact that she's refusing to tell us isn't very smart. It's odd but that might be the only thing in her favour. A guilty person would have a good story all mapped out."

"Hi Bob, is that you?" she spoke into the phone. "Listen you know that night you picked me up and we went out for a drink... What do you mean what night? I'm sorry I'm not making sense, I'm a bit agitated. Last Thursday, you remember, we had that meal... Well my car was sighted by a murder victim's house. Obviously it's not mine. It's just a mistake... No I've not dropped you in it but I can't cover up for you forever... Never mind your bloody wife, what about me!" She slammed down the receiver.

The next day DC Barnes informed Josephine that a barman at the Red Lion by the name of Phil Coombes had remembered chatting to the young man found murdered in Cockington Woods. He told him that he'd come to Torquay looking for work, apparently a friend had something for him but he'd let him down and nothing had come of it so he was returning to the Midlands the following day. Early in the evening the pub was very quiet and he'd had a good chat with him to pass the time. As it started to fill up and he became busy he didn't speak to him again. He recalled seeing him chatting to a woman with long dark hair at the far end of the bar, and they left together in a red car. "

"How did he know they'd left in a red car if he was busy serving?" Josephine asked.

"He said he'd just gone outside for a quick cigarette as the boss didn't like him smoking behind the bar. He said the woman wore a very short skirt, and had long legs and he'd found her quite fanciable himself. Apparently there were only a handful of cars in the car park as most of the locals walked to the pub," DC Barnes informed her.

"We might have her this time, it's too much of a coincidence. Get a warrant for Susan James's arrest, I want her brought into the station, and arrange an identity parade; we'll get some other women in that look similar, and let's see if this barman can pick her out."

Susan James was in a state when she arrived at the station. She was shouting.

"It's wrong I'm innocent I tell you, why won't anyone believe me?"

She screamed and kicked out as the two WPCs put her in a cell.

Phil Coombes walked along the line of women slowly looking at each one carefully. Then he went back to the office with DI Blake and DS Hughes.

"To be perfectly honest I can't say it's any of them. Number six, her eyes looked familiar and yet I couldn't swear it was her. There was something different about the other woman, she was bigger somehow. I'm sorry I can't be of more help," Phil Coombes said a little disappointed. Number six in the line up was Susan James. They thanked him for his time and he left. Josephine turned to Bill Hughes.

"He said her eyes looked familiar, there's still a chance it was her. Maybe she wore different make-up on that evening. It can alter a woman's appearance considerably."

"If only we could get more proof, anything we could tie up," Bill said anxiously.

"I'm still not sure," Josephine began, "I mean she only lives in Chelston, why pick a man up in a bar at Cockington right on your doorstep. The chances are high of seeing someone you know, especially in a local pub and why take your car, it's too close to home. I'm not sure she's the murderer."

"Well at least she's the prime suspect," Bill added. Just at that moment DC Fletcher entered the office.

"I'm sorry to interrupt but the Chief wants to see you ma'am."

"OK I'll be right down," she replied.

"Well, have you charged her yet?" the Chief Inspector asked.

"Not yet sir."

"Why ever not? All the facts point to it. We've got to get a result. The public's getting edgy."

"I've got four days left before you take me off the case," Josephine informed him.

"Well... yes... but if you got a result it would look good

on your record."

"I'm not making an arrest until I'm sure. We'd look incompetent if we had the wrong person. The press would have a field day. Just give me the time that's left, I need to be certain."

"As you wish, it's your career Detective Inspector."

When she arrived back at the incident room DS Hughes met her.

"Susan James is asking to speak to us," he informed her.

"Do you think she's ready to make a statement or confession?" she asked.

"No, I think she might have something else to tell us."

As Susan James walked into the room Josephine had that feeling again that she'd seen her somewhere before. If only she could remember where!

"You wanted to talk to us?"

"Yes that's right."

"Would you like some tea?" Josephine asked.

"Thank you, but there's no need to use the softly softly approach. I've made my mind up to tell you."

"What were your whereabouts last Thursday, when Sylvia Gordon was murdered?" Josephine inquired.

"I was out for the evening with a man. I can't divulge his name because he's married."

"So you'd rather protect him and his wife than yourself?" Josephine asked.

"What do you mean?"

"Well he'll have to give us a statement to corroborate your story."

"I doubt if he'd do that."

"Then all I can say is he doesn't think much of you Susan.

If he'd see you accused of murder, several murders in fact, just to protect his own reputation…"

"Look, I always used to leave my car at home when we went out together. I'd walk to the shops at Chelston Village and he'd meet me there, or sometimes on the sea front."

"But you're divorced aren't you?" DS Hughes asked.

"Yes that's correct."

"So surely you don't have to hide your affair from anyone. He could collect you from home," he suggested.

"It was his suggestion. He didn't want to come to my house in case someone noticed him."

A typical selfish man! Josephine thought to herself *They want extramarital sex, but none of the complications that go with it.*

"Your car was also seen about a month ago at a pub in Cockington, The Red Lion."

"I've never been in that pub, you must be mistaken," Susan James replied.

"Although in the identity parade the barman didn't positively identify you, he said you looked similar to the woman he'd seen leaving with the young man that was murdered," DS Hughes informed her.

"Well it definitely wasn't me! I keep a diary, I can tell you the days that I see… er, the gentleman in question."

"If we can see the diary and check the dates that would be a help," Josephine suggested. Susan James gave her permission for her house key to be taken from her personal effects, and told them exactly where her diary was. Half an hour or so later DS Hughes arrived back at the station with the diary. On the dates that the four murders occurred Susan James had been meeting a man called Bob. The diary appeared to be quite genuine and it was tested by the forensic department to make sure that the information hadn't been filled in at a later date.

"She appears to have a perfect alibi, if she gives us his name and it checks out," DS Hughes said.

"It's uncanny though," Josephine said thoughtfully as she looked through the diary. "She only sees him once or twice a week; how fortunate that she was with him on the exact days that the murders occur. You'd think there would be a least one that didn't tie up."

After another interview and some gentle persuasion, they finally got Susan James to give the name of the mysterious man she was dating. It was Bob Jenkins! He had also dated Caroline Ryan, and had chatted DC Fletcher up at the Blue Forest. If he hadn't seen Susan James on the nights in question he would have been a viable suspect. Unless of course they were in it together which would make them both suspects. Susan James was questioned again

"So you're prepared to sign a statement to the effect that on the nights in question you met Bob Jenkins and went out in his car."

"Yes of course, it's a fact."

"So where was your car?" Josephine asked.

"I used to leave it on my front drive."

"You didn't put it away. I notice you have a garage at the side of your house," DS Hughes commented.

"I'd never get it in there, it's full of gardening equipment and an old three piece suite that I'm getting upholstered. I've not used it for the car for at least a year."

"Do you have a spare set of car keys?"

"No just the one, why?"

"If you're not using your car, then obviously someone else is. Can you think of anyone who's borrowed it in the past?" Josephine asked.

"Well there's my brother, and my friend, occasionally I've lent them the car, but I'm sure they wouldn't take it without my permission."

"We'll have to speak to Bob Jenkins, so he can confirm what you have told us," DS Hughes informed her.

"Can you get him to come into the station, rather than go to his home?" she asked.

"You're determined to protect him at all costs, even though you're in a precarious position, still I suppose that can be arranged if you can help us out," Josephine replied.

"What do you want me to do?"

"I want you and Bob Jenkins to go out again, on one of your usual days. He's to pick you up where he normally does, and let your brother, friends, neighbours anyone you can think of know. Leave the car in the usual place on the drive, and we'll have your house under surveillance to see if anyone comes for the car."

Bob Jenkins entered the interview room.

"We've already had to question you about your relationship with Caroline Ryan who was the first victim and now we find you're involved with Susan James," DI Blake said curtly.

"My private life is my own affair," he answered.

"Not when your lady friends are connected with the murders, it's not," she snapped "You even chatted one of our DCs up at the Blue Forest when she went to make enquiries."

"I didn't know she was a policewoman," he replied.

"Obviously not otherwise I doubt if you'd have suggested those things to her," DS Hughes commented. They showed him a list of dates and he looked through them.

"I'd have to check my diary, but as far as I can tell I did go out with Susan on those days."

"How come you always insisted she left her car at home and went in yours?" DS Hughes enquired.

"Well it was safer to use mine. I'd meet her somewhere away from her house."

"I can't understand that. I mean she's divorced, so there's no jealous husband to contend with," DS Hughes commented.

"I didn't want my car seen by her house," he replied.

"Did you take her home?"

"Sometimes when it was dark I'd drop her to the door and I might go in, if it wasn't late, or she'd get out perhaps by the shops and walk the rest of the way home."

"If Susan James was found to be guilty of the murders, then you could be charged as an accomplice," DI Blake warned him.

"Look, she's innocent, she was with me I tell you, the date of the last murder, what was it?" They informed him of the date and time on the Thursday evening. "Yes well we went to a pub in Brixham, we spent the entire night there, because I won the jackpot on the fruit machine, but it paid out in tokens which you could only use in the pub on drinks. We never left till closing time. I'm sure they'd confirm my story, because they said no-one had won the jackpot in months, they're bound to remember me."

"So you spent all night drinking and then drove home," DS Hughes said.

"Yes that's right,"

"Lucky you weren't breathalysed, don't you know it's illegal to drink and drive?" Bob Jenkins didn't answer.

"I want you to continue to meet Susan James, as you have in the past, so we can watch her house, to see if anyone uses her car."

"I don't know, I was thinking of cooling it a bit." he hesitated for a moment.

"If you don't help us Mr Jenkins, things will get worse, and we may need to inform your wife."

"I'll do whatever you want," he agreed.

"Do you think they're telling the truth?" DS Hughes asked Josephine.

"Well even the neighbours confirm her car's always on the drive, although none of them have seen anyone else using the car. What day is she due to see Bob Jenkins again?"

"This Thursday," Bill informed her.

"Right, we'll get a surveillance team positioned in areas close to the house. We've told her not to let anyone know she's a suspect in case whoever's using the car gets to know."

Chapter 23

THAT THURSDAY EVENING Susan James left her house at the usual time of seven-thirty and walked to the nearby shops to meet Bob Jenkins. The police cars were situated in various places. One was positioned down a driveway, and although hidden, had a good view of Susan James's car, and the other was parked at the end of the road. They didn't use squad cars so as not to draw attention. DI Blake sat in a car nearby with DC Barnes, and DS Hughes was positioned in a nearby car park. It was eight-thirty although it was still light, being summer, and nothing had happened. Josephine was getting pretty despondent. She watched as a tall woman with long black hair walk down the road. Her heart started to beat faster, as she became excited, but the woman walked past the house. Josephine felt mortified; she couldn't remember a time when she was more disappointed but as the woman had gone about fifty yards down the road, she stopped, turned and went back the way she had come. On reaching Susan James's house, she looked around for a moment or so, and then got something out of her handbag; it was a set of keys. In a matter of seconds she had opened the car door and had reversed off the drive; she drove up the road. DI Blake radioed to the other two cars,

"You follow first Bill, make sure she doesn't see you and I'll stay behind your car." The woman drove the red Fiesta at quite a speed, but DS Hughes managed not to lose her. She went down a lane until she came to the seafront at Torquay and headed towards Paignton. They followed the car until it stopped just outside the town on a pub car park.

"Do you want us to apprehend her or see where she goes?" Bill spoke over the police radio to Josephine.

"I think the fact that she's taken the car is proof enough, we don't want to take the chance of someone else being killed; I'll follow her."

The woman got out of the car, and straightened her short skirt, she took out a compact and appeared to be checking her appearance, and after closing her bag she started to walk across the car park. Josephine followed behind her with DC Barnes; just before she reached the entrance to the pub, she said

"Excuse me, but I do believe that's not your car you've just taken."

The woman turned round; her face looked shocked and agitated. She started to run towards the road, even with high heels on she ran like the wind. Josephine and Barnes pursued her, followed by the two other cars. She made her way onto the beach, and she stumbled, breaking the heel of her shoe; kicking them off she continued barefoot, running even faster, with Barnes and Josephine chasing after her. The police cars stopped and the occupants joined the pursuit. DC Barnes who was young and fit was running with such determination; the only thought in his mind was *she mustn't get away*. This notion pumped up his adrenaline, which increased his speed.

The gap between them was finally becoming closer. He had to make a quick decision. If he dived now would he be able to stop her. He chanced it and pounced. They both went crashing to the ground. She kicked frantically in a bid to free herself from his grip. He grabbed at her hair, and to his horror it came away in his hands.

"Oh fuck it's a wig!" he shouted. He suddenly realised the made-up face was a man's as he hastily grabbed at the thighs, bringing him down again. Josephine had caught up with them by now, breathless with exhaustion.

"I know him," she gasped "It's Laurence Philby from the Blue Forest!" She realised as she stared at his face, his eyebrows and eyes were so similar to Susan James, that's why she'd kept thinking she'd seen her somewhere before. DS Hughes and the others arrived moments later and helped DC Barnes to restrain him.

"We're arresting you on suspicion of the murders of Caroline Ryan, Karen Forbes, Sylvia Gordon and Brian Jarvis; you don't have to say anything but anything you may say will be taken down and may be used in evidence against you." DS Hughes read his rights to him.

"Well done Roger!" Josephine patted Barnes on the shoulder. Laurence Philby was paying no attention to what they were saying.

"Can I've my wig back please?" he asked DC Barnes. "And look what you've done to my stockings. They were really expensive," he said as he tried to hide the ladders in them. As they handcuffed him Josephine Blake looked at him and felt repelled and sick.

"Don't you know the grief and misery you've brought to so many people's lives and all you're concerned about is your bloody stockings, you pervert!"

"I take pride in the way I dress. Every decent woman has to nowadays," he replied.

"For God's sake take him away!" Josephine said disgustedly. As they led him back along the beach to the police cars, all he prattled on about was his broken high-heeled shoes.

Chapter 24

IT TURNED OUT that Laurence Philby was Susan James's brother, which explained the resemblance Josephine had noticed. She recalled that day they visited the Blue Forest Club, and noticed how shapely his eyebrows were. He'd plucked and shaped them regularly so they blended in with his make-up. Unbeknown to Susan James, he had taken her car keys one day and got a duplicate set cut. He knew what nights she would be meeting Bob Jenkins and used her car to commit the murders and return it before she got home, which would normally be the early hours of the morning. The forensics had examined the car, and found several synthetic hairs, obviously from the different wigs he'd worn. They also found traces of the pink candlewick bedspread from Caroline Ryan's flat. They obtained a warrant, and went to search his flat above the club.

When they entered the bedroom, the bed was covered in silk underwear, stockings and tights. One small wardrobe in the room held men's clothes and the other two which were quite large were full to the brim with women's clothing. Evening dresses, suits, blouses everything you could possibly imagine. Standing on a nearby shelf were white polystyrene heads with wigs on each one, they were all colours and styles. Needless to say the room also contained an abundance of jewellery and make-up.

"He must have some money, all these are designer labels," Josephine said as she sifted through the clothes.

"The day we were here, I thought the underwear on the bed belonged to his girlfriend. I'd no idea it was his," she remarked picking up a most attractive red silk nightie.

"I told you he wasn't right didn't I?" Bill remarked.

"Yes but you thought he was gay. Even you didn't know he was a transvestite," she replied. "He may still have slept with women. I mean there are many happily married men who are straight but just need to dress in women's clothes."

As they opened the door of the other bedroom they were greeted by the sight of hundreds of teddy bears of every conceivable shape and colour you could imagine. They all had such human expressions, and looked so cuddly and sweet, like every child's dream. It was hard to believe that they had been left at the scene of such horrific crimes.

It was quite obvious to everyone that Laurence Philby was a transvestite, but still not clear why he'd committed the crimes. Dr Andrew Blythe came into the station the next day, to sit in at the interrogation.

"You were right about it being a man," Josephine said. "Well a man's body with a woman's mind and clothes, so you were partly correct in your assumption."

Laurence Philby only agreed to make a statement if some make-up and a wig was brought in for him, as he said he felt bare without them. Dr Blythe advised them to consent to his request, because he felt that if Laurence Philby felt comfortable about his appearance he would be more likely to co-operate, so they agreed. Josephine sat opposite Philby. He wore a long dark wig and his make-up was very professionally applied. He looked as attractive as any woman. His solicitor sat next to him, and DS Hughes, DC Barnes and Dr Blythe were also present. They started the tape.

"Did you murder Caroline Ryan, Mr Philby?" DI Blake asked him.

"Yes I did," he admitted. They were a little taken back he had confessed so readily.

"She was actually the cause of it all, I'd known Caroline since I was very young, I was about thirteen I think. I loved my teddy bears, I'd been collecting them for years, since I was a child. I'd been given them for birthdays and Christmas presents. I'd even got a Steiff Bear, they were made in Germany, one of the best you can get," he said remembering his youth. His eyes had a dreamy far away look to them. His face then turned from a childlike innocent expression to one of vile hatred.

"She came in one day, and caught me dressing up in my sister's clothes and she threatened to tell my parents and my friends. I couldn't have allowed her to do that. They'd have ridiculed me. She said the only way she'd keep quiet was if I gave her my collection of bears. I loved them and she took them all away. She didn't really want them, but she knew how important they were to me."

"What did your parents say when they noticed them missing?" Josephine asked.

"I told my mother and father I'd grown out of them, and didn't want to keep the bears as they were childish, so I'd given them away to friends. They were furious, and said if I hadn't have wanted them I should have given them to my sister Susan, because some were very valuable. If only they'd have known, how I hated to let them go." He started to cry.

"I can see it must have been very upsetting for you," Josephine said sympathetically.

"What made matters worse was she still told my parents, about six months or so later, and my friends as well. I was always quite tall and good at sports in school; the boys and girls made life hell for me and I had to move. I used to be admired. After she'd told them I was ridiculed and hated by everyone. My mother was quite sympathetic and suggested to my father I should get professional help, but he wouldn't hear of it; he said it was a disgrace, and if ever his work colleagues found out about me he would be so ashamed. He was an ex-army man you know. It got so bad we had to leave home. I'd loved Devon and the sea. We went back to the city. My father died of a heart attack about a year later, and although my mother had been quite sympathetic and understanding as soon as father died she blamed me and said it was the shock that killed him. For some reason they managed to keep it from Susan, she was only young at the time. When we were both older we moved back to Devon. We've never been that close, I only saw her occasionally. It wasn't until Caroline turned up at the club that the memories came flooding back. She didn't recognise me, but I knew her even though it had been years, she hadn't changed that much. I'd never forget that face that I loathed. She couldn't be allowed to get away with it; I'd acquired another collection of teddy bears over the years, but they could never replace the ones she'd taken from me. You see when I'd murdered her I left her a teddy bear, she deserved it as she'd paid for it with her life. I knew her friend from work gave her a lift home, had long dark hair and wore a blue suit, I watched her go in, so I went home and put my brunette wig on, and found a suit similar to the one she was wearing. I've got some nice clothes don't you think?" He looked at Josephine.

"I bet there were a few outfits in my wardrobe you'd kill for," he started to stroke his wig.

"It suits me this dark wig don't you think, it matches my dark eyes."

"What I can't understand," said Dr Blythe, "Karen Forbes' murder was such a frenzied attack and so messy, not your usual method of neatly displaying the bodies and tying a bow around their necks after you've strangled them."

He was trying to flatter him.

"That murder was on the spur of the moment. I'd visited the restaurant for a nice quiet evening away from the club and was sitting in an alcove enjoying my meal and a glass of wine. I overheard this woman boasting to the women she was with about how she'd got something over this chap at work, something about him being dishonest or another woman; I couldn't quite grasp what she meant. She threatened to expose him if he didn't agree to her demands. She sounded just like Caroline all those years ago. She was a repulsive, evil woman! That poor man, he might have to go through the same ordeal as me. I couldn't let her get away with it. I couldn't bear to hear her voice any longer, she'd ruined my meal. I left the restaurant but waited for her. When she'd left her friends I followed her round to the harbour. She deserved what she got. I'd done the man a favour, getting her off his back."

"Why send the teddy bear wreath to her funeral?"

"I hadn't got a teddy bear with me, so I took one back later and dropped it on the boat but he fell in the water, poor little chap. She didn't deserve anything better. She was nothing more than a blackmailer but I mean the papers said she'd got children. I sent the bear made from flowers for them. I don't suppose they'd got a teddy bear, having a mother like that."

"So what did Sylvia Gordon do?" DS Hughes asked.

"Nothing really, we were friends. I'd meet her now and again. She didn't know I was a man. I take these special hormone treatments to keep my skin smooth so I don't need to shave," he said stroking his face proudly.

"She thought I was just one of the girls, as I was always fully dressed when I met her. We went on shopping sprees together. Frankly she pissed me off, clothes always looked better on her, I always felt gawky next to her and I loved her hair and anyway by this time I was starting to enjoy killing. Mind you she put up a fight. I was wearing false nails at the time. It was a shame I marked her face. Still, I left her one of my most expensive bears to compensate. Of course the chap she was seeing Richard Myers, his wife had blonde hair, bleached job mind you. I'd taken my blonde wig so I wore it as I was leaving. I'm not keen on blonde hair and yet it looked striking with my dark eyes." He looked into Josephine's face.

"You've got nice eyes," he commented.

"Why did the young man have to die?" she asked him, ignoring his compliment.

"I'd put a lovely outfit on that night, my short red mini. I knew Susan was seeing Bob Jenkins—he's married you know. Frankly I don't know what she sees in him. So I borrowed the car, I was in this pub. And he started to chat me up."

"Is that why you dress as a woman, to attract men?" DS Hughes asked him.

"Not at all, I don't fancy men. I've always had a normal sex-life. I'm not gay, and yet I must admit I did get a certain kick from him flirting with me. I must have done a good job with my hair and make-up, he had no idea I was a man. We left together and he tried it on, I didn't want to kill him, but once he'd taken my pretty black silk pants off and seen my penis I had no choice."

"Why did you leave the note at Sylvia Gordon's house?"

"I couldn't understand why you hadn't found his body, I killed him the day or so after Caroline. Did you like the Teddy Bears' Picnic? He deserved it, he hadn't done any harm, his only mistake was thinking I was a real woman, and fancying me and you can't blame him for that."

Josephine was in the incident room thanking Bill, Sally and Roger and all the team for their hard work and support when the Chief Inspector came in.

"Well done, I knew you'd crack it!"

"Did you Chief? I don't think so. In fact I don't believe you had any faith in me at all."

He looked embarrassed.

"Anyway well done all of you, if you come over to the pub later the drinks are on me."

They were all leaving when Andrew Blythe came over to Josephine.

"Perhaps we could go for a quiet meal, purely social of course, not to discuss the case," he said his blue eyes smiling at her.

"Well Andrew, that's very flattering and tempting but I'm afraid I've got a marriage that needs working at, so I'll have to decline."

She grabbed her coat and went outside, needing some fresh air. There standing on the corner was Tom waiting for her.

"Fancy a picnic on the beach?"

"How did you know that's just what I need?" She linked her arm in his.

"Oh by the way darling, I've got something that will really improve our time in bed together."

"What's that?" he asked in anticipation. She reached into her bag.

"A book on how to stop snoring!"

The End